"**Y**our skin is

He was so close to Sharron that she had to tilt her head back. The towel on her head began to slip, and she made a grab for it a moment too late, just as it unwound and fell from her hair. The long, damp strands tumbled down her back, making her shiver.

Griff touched his finger to a long strand that curled along her shoulder. The curl straightened, then wound around his finger as though attracted to something male. Griff smiled and tucked the strand behind her ear, then drew his finger across the bridge of her nose and down to her chin. "You're still wet, you know," he said softly, catching a drop of moisture with his finger and bringing it to his lips. "Want some help drying off?"

She moaned, wondering how it would feel to have his hands on her bare shoulders. . . .

WHAT ARE *LOVESWEPT* ROMANCES?

They are stories of true romance and touching emotion. We believe those two very important ingredients are constants in our highly sensual and very believable stories in the LOVESWEPT line. Our goal is to give you, the reader, stories of consistently high quality that may sometimes make you laugh, sometimes make you cry, but are always fresh and creative and contain many delightful surprises within their pages.

Most romance fans read an enormous number of books. Those they truly love, they keep. Others may be traded with friends and soon forgotten. We hope that each LOVESWEPT romance will be a treasure—a "keeper." We will always try to publish

*LOVE STORIES YOU'LL NEVER FORGET
BY AUTHORS YOU'LL ALWAYS REMEMBER*

The Editors

625

RAISING HARRY

VICTORIA
LEIGH

BANTAM BOOKS

NEW YORK · TORONTO · LONDON · SYDNEY · AUCKLAND

RAISING HARRY

A Bantam Book / July 1993

*If you would be interested in receiving protective vinyl covers for your
Loveswept books, please write to this address for information:*

Loveswept
Bantam Books
P.O. Box 985
Hicksville, NY 11802

ISBN 0-553-44400-X

Published simultaneously in the United States and Canada

*Bantam Books are published by Bantam Books, a division of Bantam Dou-
bleday Dell Publishing Group, Inc. Its trademark, consisting of the words
"Bantam Books" and the portrayal of a rooster, is Registered in U.S. Patent
and Trademark Office and in other countries. Marca Registrada. Bantam
Books, 666 Fifth Avenue, New York, New York 10103.*

ONE

"Beam me up, Scotty."

"We're losing power, Captain. I canno' know if we have enough for the transporter."

"Do your best. Kirk out."

The garden trowel slipped from Sharron's fingers and fell to the fuchsias at her knees. There was only one explanation for the voice she was hearing: Somewhere between the lilies and alyssum, she'd discovered another dimension.

She couldn't remember the last time she'd found more than flowers or weeds in her garden.

Focusing on the three-foot-high stone wall that provided a token barrier between her property and the next, Sharron held her breath and waited.

"To the Batmobile, Robin."

"But what about the Joker, Batman?"

Sharron blinked and pushed her fingers into her long, curly blond hair before she remembered those same fin-

1

gers were coated with mulch and soil. She winced in disgust, momentarily distracted. Figures, she thought. She'd just washed her hair an hour earlier, and was letting it dry in the afternoon sun. Now she'd have to do it all over again. The flicker of annoyance was squelched by the voices behind the wall.

"There'll be another time, Robin. For now, though, Gotham City needs us."

She recognized the dialogue but not the accent. One thing she knew for certain: Neither Captain Kirk of the Starship Enterprise nor the Caped Crusader was on the other side of that wall, dimensional shift notwithstanding. Cautiously, she rose to her feet and picked her way through the clumps of flowers. It was time to confront the voices.

"Three . . . two . . . one . . . and we have lift-off!"

Sharron yelped and leapt aside as something whizzed past her left ear. Her feet landed in the petunias, and she watched in astonishment as the projectile burrowed into a cluster of begonias. She considered the advantages of retreating, but curiosity won out.

Pausing first to recover the thing from the begonias— it was a miniature rocket, black nose and silver wings with NASA stenciled on the fuselage—she resumed her advance. Tiptoeing across the last few feet of freshly turned soil, she leaned across the low wall and looked down into a pair of china-blue eyes. Child's eyes, she realized, noting the thatch of blond hair that stuck out from beneath a San Francisco Giants baseball cap before dropping her gaze to his small body. A tank top in bring pink, neon-yellow shorts that fell to his knees, and Day-Glo green high-top sneakers assaulted her incredulous stare. She had to blink twice to clear the glare from her eyes.

He probably glowed in the dark. *He*, she mused, her lips curving into a faint smile. She knew more about kids than she gave herself credit for. Her smile faded as she remembered the rocket.

"You should be more careful with your toys," she said, her gaze sliding past the child in search of an accomplice. No one. He obviously worked alone. But where had he come from? She knew for a fact that he didn't live in the house that sat on the property behind hers. That belonged to the Andersons, a retired couple whose children had all grown up and moved away from home. And the Andersons were presently away on vacation.

This was definitely a case of trespassing. Sharron found herself reappraising the boy staring up at her. "You almost hit me with that thing."

"Sowwy." His lower lip extended in a classic gesture of remorse.

Sowwy? From a child who could hold up both sides of a dialogue single-handedly? Sharron shook her head—checking for loose parts—and wondered which dimension she'd stumbled into now. She sat down on the wall, wrapping her arms around her raised knee without letting go of the rocket.

"How old are you?" She felt at a disadvantage for having to ask, but she was hampered by a fundamental ignorance of children. Thanks to a childhood spent almost exclusively studying the piano followed by eight years in the rarefied atmosphere of the concert circuit, her own guess might be skewed by as much as three years. A six-year-old, she reasoned, should be able to find his way home. Quickly, so that she could get back to gardening. Or go inside and wash her hair again.

"Three and a half." The boy held out three pudgy fingers, then four, a puzzled look overtaking his face as he tried to execute something in between. Sharron was wondering what he'd do about it when he asked, "How old are you?"

"Twenty-nine," she said without thinking, then shot him a look of disbelief followed by a scowl. Cheeky little devil, she thought, forcing back a giggle. She continued to scowl until she noticed his grin and realized he wasn't in the least bit intimidated, so she let it go with a sigh.

"Three years old," she mused aloud, wondering what she was supposed to do now. A toddler. Her expectations for a quick solution were rapidly disintegrating.

"Three and a half." He grinned even wider. "You have any kids?"

Sharron shook her head absently, her thoughts on what she was supposed to do with him.

"Why not?"

"Why not what?" she asked.

"No kids. Why not?"

"Because I don't want any." The words were out before she realized how harsh they sounded. No matter, she told herself. It wasn't as if it was any of his business.

Apparently, he wasn't of the same opinion. "You don't like kids?"

She stared at him, bemused by his persistence. Were

all children so . . . impertinent? she wondered. Still, Sharron felt compelled to answer. "It's not that I don't like children. It's just that I've never been around any. I've been content living without . . ."

She let her voice trail off as she realized she was trying to justify a very private decision to a total stranger. A three-and-a-half-year-old stranger.

She scowled again. "Where do you live?"

Not really expecting an answer, she was surprised when the boy pushed himself to his feet and pointed. Sharron's gaze followed in the direction his finger was leveled, but she saw only more of the stone wall that ran between all the homes on this block. After twenty or so yards, even that landmark disappeared, swallowed up by the trees and bushes that crowded against it.

"How far?" she asked without much hope.

He shrugged and dropped his hand, his lips parting in another grin that revealed a gap in the upper row of teeth. "I'm on a venture."

"You mean an *ad*venture, right?" She grinned back at him, pleased that she'd understood.

His head bobbled in excitement. "That wall's fun. It's long."

No kidding. She knew for a fact that it went on for several hundred yards. Pushing aside the temptation to send him back the way he'd come, she sighed and made a command decision. "I guess we'll have to find out where you belong, won't we?"

" 'Pose so." He lifted his arms in a gesture that signaled his willingness to go wherever she wanted to take him. For a moment, panic clenched at her heart. Then anger. She was a total stranger. He wasn't supposed to trust her, much less go with her. He was supposed to scream and run away, not climb into her arms.

His parents were going to get an earful when she caught up with them.

Tossing the toy rocket back onto her lawn, she reached over the wall and lifted him. He came into her arms as though they'd practiced this maneuver a thousand times, adjusting his body over the curve of her hip, locking his chubby arms around her neck, his fingers tangling in her hair. She gulped and encircled him with her own arms as he snuggled his face against her shoulder.

She suspected he was wiping his nose on her shirt. As revolted as she was by that thought, she didn't give in to the impulse to put him down.

If she let him walk, he'd likely destroy her garden. Besides, even though she couldn't see where she was going over the bulk of his small body, he was . . . warm. She ended up mashing to death three petunias and two mounds of white alyssum before reaching the security of the lawn. She spared a quick grimace for the damage, then reminded herself that summer was in its early days yet. Replacement plants would take hold and fill in with more enthusiasm now than had this happened a month later.

Clumps of dirt clung to her shoes as she strode across the lush green expanse of Kentucky bluegrass. She considered putting the boy back on his feet, but rejected the idea. On his stubby little legs, it would take twice as long to get there if she let him walk. The faster she got him inside, the sooner she could discover where he belonged.

She accidentally brushed her cheek across the brim of his cap and considered the matter closed.

The French doors that led to her living room stood open. Sharron kicked off her shoes before crossing the threshold, then zipped through the sunlit room—past the plush tropical-patterned sofa and matching armchairs, past the brass and glass coffee table, past the recently installed entertainment center, past the mahogany desk and silk-upholstered chair, and, most importantly, past the grand piano which stood in solitary splendor on an antique Persian rug at one end of the room.

It was not, she thought with a shiver of apprehension, a room designed with a child in mind. But then, children had never figured into any of her plans.

She pushed through the café-style doors to the kitchen and plopped the boy down on a stool beside the counter.

"Hungry." He stared at the refrigerator expressively.

"I'm not sure if I've got anything to eat that you'd like," she said, gently untangling his fingers from her hair. Making sure he wasn't going to topple over, she stepped back and ran a mental inventory of the contents of her refrigerator—yogurt, fresh veggies, and diet sodas. He probably wouldn't be interested, she thought, brushing at her wrinkled, used-to-be-white cotton shirt before remembering the dirt on her hands. She sighed and wondered if she dared wash up before calling the cops. Probably not. If it were her child that was missing, every second would seem like a lifetime until he was found.

"I like everything," he said.

She couldn't help the smile that pushed at the corners of her lips. "Even *I* know that kids don't like everything."

"I do." He chewed on his lower lip, and Sharron could have sworn she heard his stomach rumble. Guilt tore at her as she remembered her priorities. Call first, feed after.

"I have to make a call first. Stay there," she admonished, wagging a finger in his face before turning her back to reach for the phone.

That was her first mistake. Not the finger. Turning her back.

She looked up the number and dialed the sheriff's office. A deputy answered her call and rewarded her with good news. The boy's father had just reported him missing. The father was presently out scouring the trees and bushes, and a police car had been dispatched to the neighborhood. She hung up reassured. The northern California town was small, so it wouldn't take five minutes before the father learned where his son was to be found. Another two or three before he showed up at her doorstep. That was one of the things she liked about living in Wagner. Its size gave her a sense of security that she'd never found while living in San Francisco.

Sharron was musing over the niceties of small-town life when she turned around to ask the boy if he wanted a carton of yogurt. She found an empty stool where there should have been thirty pounds of child.

Her heart fell to her stomach. "I've lost him," she whispered, her gaze darting around the small kitchen. There wasn't anywhere to hide, not even if you were a little boy.

She took a deep breath to control the panic, then sprinted around the corner to the front door. Locked. At least he wasn't wandering around in the street. Which left only her home and the backyard.

Her definitely *not* child-proofed home.

"Where are you . . . ?" Her voice trailed off as she realized she didn't know his name. There was a three-and-a-half-year-old boy in her home, and she couldn't even call for him to come away from all those breakable things she kept well within his reach.

She changed her tactics. "Don't break anything!" she said loudly, then charged into the living room, her gaze quartering the room in desperation.

Nothing. Not a sign that he'd been in there at all . . . which, in itself, was a good sign, she imagined.

It occurred to her that he might be hiding from her, playing hide-and-seek. She hoped.

She had to find him. One house, one boy. No problem. She glanced through the windows and didn't see him out back. Then she went through the house room by room, opening closets, checking under beds, looking behind doors and calling out, "Little boy"—a phrase which sounded stupid even to her ears.

Her heart thudded in her chest, and she began to worry. Had he hidden himself in a place where he could get hurt? What if he was hiding because he *didn't* want to be found? After all, she had called the cops. Was he afraid he'd get into trouble when his dad came?

She'd make sure he didn't. Well, not too much. After all, he was only three.

Three and a half.

It was nearly a century later—about five minutes by the clock on the wall—when she spotted Day-Glo green sneakers sticking out from beneath the full-length curtains of the window behind the piano. Her heart slowed to something close to its normal rhythm as she crossed the room and pulled aside the concealing fabric.

Blue eyes shone up at her. "Your turn." He covered his eyes with his hands and began to count. "One, two, three . . ."

Sharron knelt down and pulled his hands away from his eyes. "I don't think we should play that again."

His disappointment was palpable. "You don't want to play with me?"

She decided on a change of subject and hoped his father would show before much longer. Her nerves were just a bit stretched. Settling more comfortably on the thick Persian rug, she pulled the boy away from the wall to sit in front of her.

"What's your name?" she asked when he quit squirming.

"Harry."

"Harry what?"

"Harry Ross."

The legs of the grand piano were just a few feet away, and he scooted across the rug to touch the gleaming mahogany. Sharron watched as he stroked the solid wood with his tiny hands and wondered what he'd do if he crawled onto the bench and saw the expanse of white and black keys.

Would he stroke . . . or pound? Pound probably. Didn't all kids?

He looked at her over his shoulder. "What's your name?"

"Sharron Capwell," she said, then added, "although I suppose that should be 'Miss Capwell' to you."

"Why?"

"Because it's more . . . proper." Her brow furrowed as she listened to what she'd just said. What was it about Harry that made her feel like a stuffy spinster?

"But I like Shawon."

Shawon? She smiled, not sure she didn't like that better too. "It's Sharron, not Shawon. Just like you say your name Harry, not Hawy."

Harry just gave her a blank look and returned his attention to the piano, crawling over to the brass pedals and giving them a tentative poke. When the doorbell rang, she judged Harry was safe where he was under the piano—and vice versa—and scrambled up from the floor.

Moving quickly, she crossed the marble entryway and opened the door. And stared.

There wasn't a single doubt this was Harry's father. It wasn't the almost straight light blond hair—just a shade or two darker than Harry's—that gave Sharron her first clue. Rather, it was the magenta-and-white rugby T-shirt worn over green shorts that authenticated the relationship between father and son. The inability to coordinate clothing was obviously an inherited trait.

There the resemblance stopped.

Where Harry was slightly chubby and soft, his father

was not. No, this man was lean and hard. She didn't have to touch him to know that . . . although her fingers itched with the temptation to do just that. Her gaze drifted over his wide shoulders, the powerful muscles clearly outlined by the knit shirt. The strength of his body made him seem tall, although she guessed he couldn't be more than five or six inches taller than her own five and a half feet.

Her gaze returned to his tanned face. Beneath what must have been nearly a week's growth of beard, the sharp contours and strong chin had an attractive appeal. She wondered if Harry's baby face would someday mature like this. She hoped so, and wished the next generation of young girls and women good luck. They'd need it with this kind of temptation in their paths.

The brown-blond beard was curiously provocative—although Sharron had never before considered herself a beard person. Did Harry's father ever shave, or was he, like herself, on vacation? Somehow, she didn't think his appearance could be improved one iota.

Unless he changed clothes. The shorts and shirt combination was an eyesore.

Then again, for a woman with dirt in her hair and under her fingernails, she didn't have much room to criticize.

She knew that she should stop staring, but she couldn't . . . not when a set of dark brown eyes was staring right back at her, doing the same sort of inventory she'd embarked on just moments before. They were intelligent eyes, amused without being derisive.

She liked them a lot.

"I'm Harry's father."

"I knew that," she said quickly, giving herself a little shake as she realized she'd been visually feasting on the man who was married to Harry's mom.

Harry's father's wife. She was probably wringing her hands as she paced the floor and waited for her husband to bring her baby home.

Sharron's color deepened at least three full shades in her mortification. It was bad enough ogling a stranger, but a *married* stranger . . . She shook her head in irritation. Married men were definitely on her list of nonplayers.

"Harry's under the piano." She stepped aside so he could get a clear view of her living room. *Nothing like making a total fool out of yourself, Sharron*, she chastised herself. Yet she dared to look at him again, and discovered his gaze hadn't moved. He was still watching her, studying her face.

Reading her thoughts.

He knew exactly what she was thinking—that she was attracted to him, that she wouldn't let herself get involved with another woman's man.

"I'm not—" he began, but she was faster.

"You look like Harry," she said, determined to ride this out with a modicum of pride.

"I do?" He laughed softly, a wonderfully masculine sound that crept up her spine and made her wish life were fair.

She shook off the mellow tingling, opting for discretion. "Your hair," she said. "Straight and blond. But your eyes—"

"Are brown," he said. "Harry's are blue."

She searched for other comparisons but came up empty. Almost. Grinning she turned and led the way into the living room. "It's probably something about the way you both dress."

She watched his bewildered gaze flit from his own clothes to those of his son, who now sat in front of the entertainment center. Harry's father glanced back at her, looking as though he doubted her sanity, then turned his attention to his son.

"Hello, Harry," he said as he hunkered down beside the small boy, sliding his arm around the tiny shoulders for a quick hug. Sharron found tears brimming her eyes at the scene, such a simple thing, a father with his son. A family. Simple, for some.

"Hi, Dad." Harry pressed a sloppy kiss to his father's cheek, then clicked the black remote control in his hand. The television burst into life.

His father gently took the remote from Harry's fist and switched off the set. "I'd like to know how you got here, Harry."

And I'd like to know how you turned on the television. Sharron had to bite her lip to keep from asking the question aloud. She'd been trying to discover how to do that ever since the entertainment center had been installed three days earlier. Now, she decided, was not the time.

She'd prefer to get it figured out without embarrassing

herself. After all, if a three-year-old could do it, so could she. Three and a half, she corrected herself. But then, kids teethed on technology these days.

"I followed the wall," Harry answered his father. He reached for the remote and puckered his lips in frustration when it was held high above his head.

"You were supposed to stay in the backyard."

"You said I could explore," Harry countered, not showing any concern that he'd miscalculated.

"I meant the backyard." Harry's dad was beginning to look resigned, perhaps already aware he'd lost on a technicality.

Harry just shrugged, the deliberately exaggerated movement nearly forcing a chuckle from Sharron. "Shawon smells good. I like her."

"Shawon?" Harry's dad's glance slid across the room to where Sharron perched on the arm of the sofa. It was her turn to shrug.

Harry pushed himself up from the floor and crossed to Sharron, poking her in the thigh with a stubby finger. "Shawon."

She decided she much preferred Shawon to Miss Capwell any day. "Sharron Capwell," she said for the older male's benefit, then smiled down at the toddler who continued to prod her thigh. With a sense of astonishment, she realized she was enjoying herself . . . and Harry.

"I guess we did forget the introductions," the man said as he rose to his full height. He took her hand in a firm clasp that made her tingle from head to foot and swallow back a gasp of pleasure so outrageous, she barely recognized it.

"I'm Griff Ross," he said, the words boring into her consciousness as she wondered whether it was Batman or Captain Kirk who'd granted this man his power to paralyze with a touch. Perhaps Spock.

She managed a short laugh and shook her head, bemused by the afternoon's increasingly bizarre chain of events. "Griff? Short for . . ."

"Griffen. One of those family names you don't hear much these days. I'm sorry if Harry interrupted anything." He let go of her, then glanced down at his hand as Harry melted away unnoticed to the nether regions of the living room.

Sharron felt her cheeks warm in embarrassment when she saw some of her garden dirt had transitioned in the handshake, but she merely folded her hands in her lap and hoped he wouldn't notice the dirt in her hair.

He did notice it, but he had the good manners not to mention it. His raised eyebrows, though, were expressive enough to make the words nonessential.

She knew her hands and hair weren't the only things he'd noticed. Griffen Ross saw everything, from her mud-streaked white blouse to the too-big, too-ratty shorts she'd worn for a private afternoon in the garden.

It wasn't as though it mattered, she told herself. To either of them.

"Harry tends to get carried away with exploring," he said, smiling. "We're new to the area, and he's determined to see everything."

Sharron suddenly remembered the panic she'd felt at Harry's excessive trust. "I'm sure he won't try it again, not if you keep an eye on him."

"I *was* watching him." His gaze narrowed on her face, nearly making her regret the implied criticism. Nearly, but not quite. If Harry's mom didn't know enough to keep a three-year-old from wandering the neighborhood, perhaps his dad needed to learn.

"So how did he get here?" she asked, conveniently forgetting her own lapse of attention which had ended in a frantic game of hide-and-seek.

"I went into the house for a Popsicle. For Harry. I assumed he'd be okay in the backyard." Griff thrust long fingers through his hair, pushing it back off his forehead. "That's why I chose Wagner when we decided to move to California. It's reputed to be a safe place to live."

"Maybe you should have talked with Harry, then," she suggested. "It frightened me when he came with me so easily. I could have been . . . anyone."

A flush that was part fear, part anger darkened his face beneath the tan, but Sharron only gave it the barest consideration. She'd noticed that Harry had moved to the coffee table where he was threatening her collection of crystal figurines. She firmly pulled his hands back from their tentative exploration, proud she hadn't panicked. Harry didn't persist, but as she was moving the crystal to a higher, safer place, he focused his attention on an intricate arrangement of silk flowers that flowed from a large vase in the corner. Shooing him away from the vase, she glanced up to notice Griffen Ross had followed her across the room.

He looked ready to explode, a condition Sharron understood. There was a turbulence inside her that was worse than any case of stage fright she'd ever known. Her senses were on full alert, her nerves jumping and trembling. And it was directly related to this man. Despite knowing he was out of reach, despite her disapproval of how he'd lost Harry and her guilt at reminding him of the consequences every parent fears . . . despite it all, something about him made her want to know him better.

Fat chance, she thought. Mrs. Ross had first option.

It probably wasn't Griffen Ross who was making her crazy anyway. It was the presence of one three-and-a-half-year old boy named Harry who was roaming her living room with mayhem on his mind. She was sure of it.

She was also sure she'd overstepped her bounds in criticizing Harry's father's parenting technique. Griffen Ross didn't seem the irresponsible type. There was the way he spoke with Harry, touched him. It was so obvious that he loved his son very much. It was just that Harry was so small. And Griff made her feel so . . . *defensive*.

Griff. A familiar name for someone who, her defensiveness aside, she felt so very familiar with.

It wasn't to be. Neighbors, yes. Friends, perhaps. But really familiar? It wasn't in the cards.

"I'm sorry, Mr. Ross," she said, shaking her head. "It wasn't my intention to worry you. It's just that . . . well, you see so many stories in the news." She didn't elaborate, keeping in mind small ears and the tragedies that were incomprehensible to most parents and horrifyingly real to others. It wasn't her place to instill a fear of strangers in this small child.

"Perhaps he's a better judge of character than you give him credit for." Griff gently nudged Harry away from the French doors where he was in the process of leaving multiple fingerprints.

Sharron thought he'd conquered his anger until he added, "It's easy for someone who doesn't have any kids to criticize. You can only teach and watch them so far. The rest is up to them." His voice was low and tight.

"How do you know I don't have any kids?" Being caught interfering was suddenly less embarrassing than imagining she looked like the type of woman who didn't have children. Was there a type? she wondered. Did she look less motherly than other women? Less caring?

He grinned, astonishing her with his sudden change in mood. "If you had any, you'd realize they're smart enough at three to know their address and phone number."

"He does?"

"He does."

Her brow furrowed as she recalled trying to get any information out of Harry. "But when I asked him where he lived, he just pointed down the wall."

"That wasn't enough?" The fact that he'd said it with a smile was all that saved him.

Sharron gave a small laugh. "Only if you live in a tree house. With Harry employing the point-the-finger-in-the-direction-of-home technique, I was led to believe he didn't know what city we're in, any more than he'd know the difference between planet Earth and your nearest space station."

"A three-year-old probably doesn't comprehend which city he's in, much less space stations versus planet Earth," he agreed. "It's all a matter of asking the right questions." He motioned to Harry and, once again, hunkered down to his son's level. "What's our address, Harry?"

"One hundred seventeen Peachtree Lane."

"And our phone number?"

"555–1420." Almost apologetically, Harry recited the number a second time for a stunned Sharron, then added, "You didn't ask me that."

"I guess I didn't," she said, deciding she'd might as well have a sign pasted on her back that read I DON'T KNOW THE LEAST LITTLE THING ABOUT CHILDREN.

It made her feel empty, even more so when Griffen Ross stood and clasped his son's hand. They were going to leave . . . leaving behind a woman who was only just beginning to comprehend what one small child could bring to her solitary life. There was a time when she'd been so confident of her choices, but now, today, it all felt wrong.

At the very least, askew.

It wasn't over, though. Not yet. Still holding his son's hand tightly within his own, Griff stepped close to her, close enough to block the view of anyone kneecap level and below.

"Thank you for being worried," he said, and when she looked into his face, she saw that he was truly grateful. It was a relief, that she hadn't overreacted, hadn't done the wrong thing. Griff moved closer, lowering his voice until his words were a mere whisper. "I love Harry, but every day I'm learning. I know I'm not a perfect father, but I'm the only one he has."

"So why are you whispering?" she asked in the same muted voice, giving a thought to Mrs. Ross and feeling such incredible envy that she had to swallow back the words that would express it. "I'm sure Harry knows you love him."

"He doesn't know I'm not perfect."

TWO

Her hair was still damp from its second washing that day as Sharron cleaned the crystal figurines, replaced them, then moved to the French doors to wipe away the fingerprints of a small boy named Harry. By the time she had everything rearranged to her satisfaction, the bright afternoon sunlight had given way to the gentler rays of dusk.

"So if I can't garden, I'll just watch TV," she said aloud, confident that she could make the proper connections. Before, she'd only played at turning on the set, mostly because she figured something was inherently wrong with it if she couldn't get it to work. But now, she took her task to heart, sitting cross-legged in front of the set with a remote control in each hand. Why there were two of the little black things was just one of the mysteries she needed to solve.

She took heart. If a child could figure it out, so could she. But Harry had at least known which of the two to use. One apparently went to the cable hookup, the other to the

TV. But which was which? Even better, which had Harry used?

An hour later, Sharron had to exercise maximum restraint to keep from tossing the electronic gadgets into the trash—*where they belonged*. Marching into the kitchen, she made a note on the refrigerator door to call the company that had installed the equipment. It was a wasted gesture, but she ignored that fact even as she wrote the note.

She *never* looked at the reminders she left on the refrigerator. Somehow, her eyes were always more interested in what was inside the appliance rather than the odd bits of paper that clung to the door. Not that there was ever anything more than yogurt or something equally as healthy inside, but she never lost the hope that gremlins would surprise her someday with a decadent treat.

Hope triggered her appetite, and she opened the door to inspect the contents within. No surprises. Sharron slammed the door and picked up the phone to order a pizza, ignoring her conscience in a rebellious mood that defied years of dieting and habit. Perhaps it was time to jettison that diet, just as she'd recently shed the career that had spawned it. The life of a concert pianist wasn't easy— weeks and months on the road with home-cooked foods a rarity, so that healthy eating habits were essential to keep up her strength.

Life on the road was over, she remembered, giving the person from the pizza place her address before hanging up. It was time to take care of herself in ways she wouldn't have considered before. Time to splurge.

Time to take a deep breath, and know it was because

she wanted to smell the roses rather than fortify herself with the nerve to perform for the crowd that waited beyond the curtains.

Time to take a new direction with her life.

Confident it would be a short wait—for the pizza, if not her new life—she opened a bottle of Chianti and carried a small glass out to the patio. Relaxing on the chaise lounge, she sipped the wine and concentrated on the subtle noises of the approaching night.

Somehow, tonight, they were louder than she remembered, the whiz and burr of insects, the rustle of leaves in the breeze. Louder, but less comforting.

Tonight, for the first time in years, Sharron felt . . . alone.

She spent the next morning with Debussy. Sometimes melancholy, sometimes just plain soothing, the composer was her cure of choice.

It didn't work, though. Not in the way it was supposed to.

Her fingers found the proper keys on the piano without thought. A good thing, too, because her thoughts were on a man she barely knew . . . and a boy she'd held in her arms like she'd held none other.

It disturbed her that it disturbed her.

Harry. Funny how she couldn't make up her mind about him. Children weren't a part of her life, never had been. She imagined they never would be. Not in the having-any-of-her-own sense.

It wasn't because she was too old. Even Sharron knew twenty-nine was still young in the scheme of things. She could wait five, even ten years before it would be risky to have a baby. Risky, but not inconceivable.

Inconceivable. Conceivable. Conceive.

The words looped together with as little effort as it took to blink her eyes. Sharron stumbled over a simple arpeggio and mentally replaced inconceivable with unthinkable. Unthought.

Children weren't something she'd thought about. Not seriously at any rate.

Unthinkable, not inconceivable. *Could she conceive?*

Unthinkable, really, and even more so in another five years. Five more years of being set in her ways. Five more years of living life in the company of adults. Five more years to confirm she wouldn't know a maternal instinct if it jumped out of the piano and bit her.

Not even a little charmer like Harry could change the assumptions of a lifetime.

The sun was high overhead by the time she gave up any pretense at knowing what she was doing at the keys of a piano that cost more than most cars. She changed into her gardening grubbies, tied her hair back with a silk ribbon, and traipsed across the lawn to her garden. Perhaps tending the posies would bring her peace.

Bring her joy.

The petunias that had had the misfortune to be underfoot the previous day were snipped, shaped, and tended. The damage was minimal. After cutting away the mashed blossoms and stems, she cultivated the ground around the plants, then poured a mixture containing liquid fertilizer into the soil.

Satisfied that she'd done everything humanly possible to mitigate the brutal treatment of the previous day, she eyed the nearby alyssum and debated whether it would pop back up on its own or if she should try surgery. She was just making a case for pulling it out altogether when she heard scrambling along the wall.

It might be a cat, she told herself before lifting her gaze to the stone wall. It wasn't, of course. But then, she really hadn't expected one.

It was Harry, arms spread wide in imitation of a tightrope walker, his tiny feet kicking at loose rocks as he slowly walked along the top of the wall.

Sharron sat back on her heels, trying not to get too involved with his acrobatics as she speechlessly watched each step that brought the toddler closer. The wall wasn't all that narrow—about eighteen inches or so across, she guessed—but it was nearly as tall as Harry. She was afraid to say anything, nervous that she might startle him.

Her tongue was dry against the roof of her mouth as she offered silent encouragement.

His bottom lip was caught between his teeth in concentration, his eyes glued to the uneven path he'd chosen. When he drew level with Sharron, he grinned, spreading his arms even wider as though she was his reward for performing that mad, bold feat.

She had no choice but to flow with it, stepping lightly through the flower bed and returning with considerably less finesse, weighted down as she was by thirty-plus pounds of child. The alyssum took another beating, but the petunias escaped. She missed those in favor of a rather straggly patch of yellow marigolds she'd never liked anyway.

Harry's chubby arms remained tightly wrapped around her neck even after they reached the grass. She should have said something, she realized, but the words of reprimand wouldn't come. Not then, not with his little body safe and warm against hers.

It was silly, she knew, but it felt good.

It felt like she should offer him words of congratulations.

"Hi, Shawon," he said into her ear, snuggling closer as though perfectly content to stay cuddled in her arms forever.

"Hello, Harry," she returned, injecting a note of sternness into her voice to hide something that felt remarkably like relief. "Don't you think that wall is a little dangerous?"

"Not if you don't fall." He tightened his legs at her waist as she attempted to put him down.

Nothing like a little logic to put one in one's place, she mused, searching for another angle to clarify the danger. She couldn't summon one and decided it wasn't her problem anyway. If his own mother couldn't figure that one out— She halted midthought.

"Does your mom know you're here?" she asked, leaning back to see his face.

The puzzled look he gave her was enough of an answer. Of course his mother didn't know. And it didn't look like Harry was willing to get into that subject, not when he'd just escaped from his own backyard again. He was supposed to know better, though.

Obviously, neither Griffen Ross nor his wife had managed to curb Harry's enthusiasm for adventure. Sighing, Sharron crossed the lawn and hoped Harry's mom would be home today. Another meeting with his dad couldn't possibly be good for her.

What kind of woman had Griffen Ross married? It was curiosity, nothing more, she told herself, that made her wonder.

Curiosity killed the cat. Sharron winced at the adage and hugged Harry tighter.

"Need my rocket." Harry nearly fell out of her arms as he twisted to look to where she'd tossed the toy missile the day before.

She gave him a startled glance. "Is that what you came back for?"

He nodded, his fingers busy tugging at the ribbon around her hair. "And the launchpad. It's over the wall."

Over the wall. Terrific. Sharron gave another sigh, then backtracked. Disentangling his fingers from the ribbon, she plopped Harry down on the grass, climbed the wall, and retrieved the launching mechanism from the Andersons' yard. The garden was less squishy underfoot than before, already inuring itself to her repeated trips between the flowers. Briefly, she considered the value of shaping a series of bricks into a footpath, but discarded it as ridiculous.

Harry wouldn't be back, not now that he had what

he'd come for. After a rather daring leap over the knee-high azalea bush, Sharron handed him the launchpad. Her heart nearly melted at the pleased-as-punch expression on his face.

A child's uncomplicated approval was not something she was accustomed to.

With a definite tightness in her throat, she picked up the rocket and held out her hand to the small boy. Together, they marched across the lawn to the patio where rocket and launchpad were deposited on the patio table.

"What's your phone number, Harry?" she asked as she kicked off her shoes, then bent to help him with his.

"Why?"

"So I can call your mom." Sharron pasted an encouraging smile on her face as Harry hesitated, obviously debating the merits of sharing this information. It wasn't until her own expression took on a relatively stern cast that he mumbled the number.

"Can I watch TV?" he asked, following her into the house.

"Please may I," she corrected him automatically, waiting expectantly for the proper version from Harry.

She didn't get it. Nor, apparently, did he.

Harry just grinned and said, "You can watch too. *Maya the Bee* is on."

Sharron stifled a giggle and handed him the two remote controls.

He handed one back to her. "You only need one."

One mystery solved. She tried to see which button he clicked, but the angle was wrong and she didn't want to make a big deal of it. Later, she promised. Certainly before he left.

She went into the kitchen and dialed the number Harry had given her. When a familiar masculine voice answered, the tension she'd been trying to ignore burst into speech.

"This is your neighbor Sharron Capwell. Harry's over here, or hadn't you missed him yet?"

"Harry's upstairs napping." He spoke with the assurance of a man who knew he was right.

"No, Mr. Ross, he's not. Harry's presently in my living room watching something about a bee." Sharron peered around the corner and was reassured by the sight of Harry sitting Indian-style in front of the television. Too close, she was sure, but it wouldn't be long enough to affect his vision on a permanent basis.

She wondered if Griffen Ross paid attention to stuff like that. Or Harry's mother.

"You're sure you've got the same kid as before?" His question drove concerns of twenty-twenty vision right out of her mind.

Her mouth gaped open in disbelief as Griffen Ross continued in support of his case. "They're kind of like squirrels, you know. Unless you know what you're looking for, they all look alike. And yesterday, I kind of got the impression you'd do better at telling squirrels apart than children."

She was tempted to hang up on him and keep the kid. For a while, anyway. At least until he taught her the magical sequence of buttons necessary to turn on the television. Squirrels indeed! Her gaze rolled over Harry's purple shirt, green shorts, and red sneakers. Of course, it was Harry. She didn't have to look at his china-blue eyes to know that. Not that she'd seriously doubted who it was. She knew much more about kids than she had this time yesterday.

Besides, Harry had given her this phone number. Satisfied, she turned her back on the noise coming from the living room.

"Sorry to disappoint you, Mr. Ross—"

"It's Griff," he interrupted brusquely. "And I'm not disappointed. I'm . . ." The deep growl trailed off as the man behind it grappled with the facts. "I'm embarrassed. He's *supposed* to be upstairs. Asleep."

Griff. She bit back a sigh and wished Harry's mom would surface before much longer. "You should probably come and get him before he breaks something," she said.

"Just tell him not to touch anything," the male voice rumbled back at her. "Simple instructions are all kids usually need. I'll be right there." He hung up, and she was left listening to a dial tone, wishing she'd walked Harry home instead of making that call. So much safer . . .

She hung up the phone and turned back to the living room, only to stumble over Harry who stood right in her path. She caught her balance on the doorjamb, barely managing to keep from squishing the toddler underfoot.

Harry, his lip stuck out in a well-defined pout, appeared not to notice her efforts not to knock him on his butt. "You don't want me here."

"I didn't say that, Harry." She knelt down until they

were practically nose to nose. "I just told your daddy to come get you. I'm sure he was worried."

Harry shook his head and reached forward to tug at the bow around her hair, succeeding this time in pulling it out. "What's to worry? He didn't know I was here till you tol' him." He twisted the ribbon in his chubby hands, the pink silk knotting between his fingers.

She suppressed a grin and shook her hair free, enjoying the tickle of it halfway down her back as she gave Harry her sternest look. "I suspect your dad won't be happy you snuck out behind his back."

"He didn't tell me not to," Harry retorted, eyeing her carefully as though he were in doubt where her allegiance lay.

It was a tough call. "I don't think you've quite grasped the essence of obedience," she said, and wasn't surprised when Harry's face scrunched in a total lack of understanding. She'd done it on purpose, she realized, used big words so that he wouldn't know what she meant.

As far as Sharron was concerned, her allegiance was still up for grabs. The doorbell rang, and she gave Harry a quick pat on the cheek before moving to answer it.

Harry's dad still hadn't shaved, and it looked as though he'd maybe thought about combing his hair but had used his fingers when he couldn't find a comb. Interesting, she thought. This man looked better tousled than most others did on their best days.

Checking out his clothing, she hoped this wasn't one of his best days. Griffen Ross sported a faded blue Seattle Seahawks T-shirt over orange knit shorts that fitted loosely around his thighs. Great legs, she thought, rationalizing that she couldn't help but look at them if she wanted to see his shoes. On his feet was a pair of sneakers that should have been trashed a hundred wearings before, his toes sticking out of holes in the sides and the rubber on the bottom looking as though it was held there by a prayer, nothing more.

The packaging was far inferior to almost anything she could imagine, yet she was captivated. Intrigued.

Appalled that she was doing it again. Staring.

And getting caught. Griff's eyes were soft with laughter as he captured her gaze. "At least *I* put on something clean," he murmured.

Mortified, she looked down at the baggy shorts and dirty shirt she'd pulled on from the day before. So much for the pot calling the kettle black. At least there wasn't any dirt in her hair. Self-consciously, she lifted a hand to her head, pushing back the heavy mass of hair as Griff watched.

When his surprisingly intense gaze returned to her eyes, she forgot about everything except for the man. She dropped her hand to her throat, covering the pulse with her fingers. *What would it be like . . . with a man like this?*

Harry's father. Harry's mother's husband. The facts, again, filled her expectations with lead.

She cleared her throat. "I wasn't expecting guests," she said, stepping back from the door and motioning him in. She was vaguely aware that the noise from the television had been absent for several minutes. She hoped Harry wasn't playing another game of hide-and-seek.

"Believe it or not, I wasn't expecting to be one." Griff passed her slowly as though reluctant to end the moment. But he did, finally, clear the doorway and walk into the living room.

Too late. For so many reasons.

The only one she'd admit to was louder than the others. A resounding crash filled the air, followed by the sound of shattering glass.

And a small child's startled scream.

Griff ran toward the noise, Sharron at his heels—heels that skidded to an abrupt stop just around the corner. She bounced against a broad back that didn't give an inch, only just managing to recover her footing as Griff moved again. Before she knew it, he was turning back to her, Harry in his arms and crying hard against his father's shoulder.

Griff set the boy down on the floor between them, and together he and Sharron did a quick inventory of his limbs. No cuts, no blood, no nothing. She double-checked the bottoms of his feet, cursing herself for taking off his shoes earlier. No problem there, either. He was breathing okay, too, or would be when the cries and hiccups stopped.

"You okay, Sport?" his father asked finally.

Harry nodded, brushing away a tear that was followed by a steady stream of the same. Sharron's heart went even softer. She figured it would be mush by the time Harry finished with it.

"You're going to be okay, Harry," Griff said just loud

enough for Harry to hear over his sobs. "That's right, cry it all out. You'll feel better in a minute."

"Scared." Harry hiccuped over the word, his little body burrowing more deeply into his father's arms. Griff held him close and stroked his hair, murmuring quiet words of love and reassurance. The two blond heads bowed together. Father and son, a blend of love even a stranger couldn't miss.

Harry was going to be okay. Sharron realized that just moments before reaction set in. Images of Harry bleeding to death filled her mind and made her grab something, anything. Griff's arm, she realized absently, but didn't let go.

The panic was extraordinary.

She'd known better than to take her eyes off Harry, but she had. Just as Griff had gone inside for a Popsicle, she'd let her attention lapse for a critical thirty seconds, maybe less.

Parenting was a whole world of its own, a world filled with terror and panic interspersed with a dose of old-fashioned worry. A world completely alien to her, and certainly not one she could see herself getting the hang of. It was a good thing she didn't have any maternal instincts.

She didn't think she'd survive if today was anything to go by.

Harry might have died.

He hadn't, though. Griff wouldn't be talking to him in that low, soothing voice, and Harry wouldn't be sniffling back his cries. The child leaned back a little, his face puffed from crying, his father's shirt wet from hundreds of tears. Even so, Sharron thought, Harry looked pretty good, especially considering the mess of broken glass and silk flowers that lay scattered just a few feet away. There were marbles, too, the ones that held the flowers straight in the vase. Used to hold them straight, she corrected herself, eyeing the shards of glass that had been a vase she would have thought was out of Harry's reach. The vase had been. The fault lay with the plant stand, she realized. Sturdy by most standards, but obviously not up to snuff when little boys were concerned. It, too, had bit the dust.

"Sowwy, Shawon." Harry peered out from the security of his dad's lap, a look of genuine regret on his face.

"It's okay, Harry." And she meant it. It was okay. He could break anything of hers as long as he didn't hurt himself. "I know it was an accident."

The small boy nodded, then wiped his nose on the back of his hand. "Accident," he confirmed, burrowing back into his father's embrace. Griff gave him a hard hug.

She wished Harry would crawl into her lap now and give her a little of that comfort he was lavishing on his father. Couldn't he see how scared she'd been?

"You can let go now, Sharron." A warm, masculine hand tugged at her fingers, pulling them away from where they'd become imbedded in his forearm. Well, almost imbedded. The tiny half-moons left by her fingernails probably weren't permanent, she mused. At least she hadn't drawn blood.

"Sorry about that," she said. "I guess I'm not very good in emergencies." She flushed brightly, embarrassed by her show of emotion.

"You did just fine," Griff said softly. "It's okay to get a little shaky afterwards."

"Really?"

He nodded. She gulped and stared at his arm, wondering what Mrs. Ross would say about the marks there. Sharron was considering flying out of state to finish her vacation when Griff snagged her hand and lifted it to where both he and Harry could study it. "It's a good thing your nails are short," he said, shifting Harry onto one leg. "You have remarkably strong fingers."

"The piano." With her free hand, she gestured toward it. Griff's gaze followed, but didn't get all the way across the room to where the grand piano stood in all its glory. Sharron knew he had only gotten as far as the pile of broken glass and ruined flowers, and by the time he turned back to her, the damage had fully registered.

He fixed her with a resigned stare and said, "You didn't tell Harry not to touch, did you?"

THREE

"Just like you didn't tell Harry not to come over here again." Sharron glared at Griff across the top of Harry's head. "Or did you?"

She got up from the floor and made a show of brushing herself off, although she was fairly certain the floor was much cleaner than her gardening clothes. Without giving Griff a chance to defend himself, she retreated to lean against the wall and said, "Does Harry's mother have any better luck keeping track of him than you do?"

Harry looked up at his father and said with a trace of concern, "Shawon's mixed-up."

Griff bit back a chuckle and dropped a kiss on his son's forehead before standing. "Not mixed-up, Harry. Just misinformed."

Misinformed? Sharron wondered as the two males stared at her with shared amusement. "You mean you *did* tell him not to come over?" What was so funny about that?

"That's another subject," Griff said, shaking his head. "The one we're on is entitled 'Harry's mom.'"

"Harry's mom?" she repeated blankly, her gaze shifting from one Ross male to the other.

Griff looked as though he was going to say something when Harry cut in. "I don't have a mom. Just a dad." He grinned and tucked his arm around his father's calf. "I'm 'dopted."

"Dopted?" Sharron blinked twice, then squinted at the duo. "You mean adopted?" But they looked so much alike . . .

Griff nodded, his hand cupping the boy's shoulder to keep him from wandering off. "We've been together three years now, ever since he was a baby."

"Three and a half," piped up Harry, earning a chuckle from his father.

"Three and a half," Sharron repeated, focusing on the facts. Harry was adopted and didn't have a mom. He only had a dad . . . who didn't have a wife.

The blush blindsided her, bringing a low, sexy laugh from Griff. Yes, she decided, sexy was the word for it.

And that was okay with her.

"No wife," Griff said clearly, holding her gaze until Harry stole his attention by trying to climb up his body, using Griff's shins as footholds. Griff grappled with the climbing boy, adding in a low voice that barely carried above the childish laughter, "So you see, Sharron, it's all right if we stare at each other and like it."

Very all right. She was still getting used to the idea when Griff asked for a broom and dustpan. She gave him both, then dashed into her room to slip into shoes before returning to help. Harry sat in the middle of the entry-way; his father was promising dire consequences if he budged. Apparently convinced the toddler wouldn't move, Griff began to sweep up the mess as Sharron picked out the flowers and laid them aside. The job was accomplished much faster than she would have expected, and she was cautiously poking through the debris for the marbles when Griff's hand clamped around hers, drawing her up from her knees.

"Don't do that. You'll cut yourself."

"But I want the marbles," she said. "All I have to do—"

"Is slice off a finger." He spread her fingers between his. "Unless, of course, you don't need all of them to play the piano?"

Her breath caught in her throat, a response to his touch. She swallowed hard and found herself wondering if she dared respond to the heat in his gaze. There was a challenge there, a dare.

An excitement was building slowly, steadily in the silence between them.

"Can I watch TV, Dad?" Harry wedged his small body between the two adults and stared up at them.

Giving her hand an extra squeeze, Griff slipped his fingers from hers and transfered his attention to his son. "I thought I told you not to move."

"You're done sweeping. I'm bored."

"So let's talk about your wall-climbing then," Griff suggested.

Sharron backed away, intending on leaving the room to give them privacy. Griff raised his head, though, and said, "Stay." He added with a half smile, "You need to see what I'm up against."

Sharron couldn't resist. She stayed, scooting a few feet away to rest her back against the sofa. Griff sat down on the floor and patted a spot in front of him where he wanted Harry to sit. Harry plopped down with an ease Sharron admired and knew she couldn't hope to imitate, ever. His lips were curved in an expectant smile, and he looked as though he were about to be entertained.

Perhaps he was.

Obviously, the kid wasn't afraid of anything. Spooked by falling vases, perhaps, but certainly not worried about anything his father might have to say.

Sharron knew who was in charge of *that* household.

"I thought we discussed these adventures yesterday," Griff began in a mild voice, returning Harry's grin as his hand closed over the child's smaller one.

"Yup."

Quirking an eyebrow, Griff checked to make sure he'd heard right. "Yup?" he repeated. "That's it?"

Harry wrinkled his brow, trying to figure out what he was supposed to say. As Sharron watched, he stumbled on the answer. His face lit up in a hundred-watt smile. "Sorry, Dad."

Sorry. Sharron hadn't missed the discrepancy. Sorry, not sowwy, as he'd said to her just minutes before. Selective pronunciation. She wondered why she'd been singled out for the adorable baby talk?

Sorry. Griff tried to keep an answering smile from his face, but only partially succeeded, ending up with a lopsided grin that Harry tried to imitate. As a reward for getting at least part of it right, Griff let Harry clown for a few moments before putting his serious face back on.

"Sorry is okay if you know you're wrong," he began, feeling his way through the potentially hazardous situation. If he was too light-handed, Harry wouldn't believe what he was saying and that could be dangerous. But, on the other hand, if he overreacted, he might crush Harry's adventurous spirit.

It wasn't easy to concentrate, not with Sharron sitting where he could see her out of the corner of his eye. Sharron, with hair halfway down her back the color of gold, hair he'd wanted to touch from the moment she'd first opened the door. Hot and cold Sharron, not knowing it was okay to be attracted, not allowing herself to react to Griff's own undeniable interest until she knew the facts. Griff liked that, her sense of right and wrong. Sharron, a woman who didn't flaunt her charms but instead hid them beneath ratty shirts and shorts. A mouth that was red without lipstick, a complexion that owed nothing to cosmetics, and clear gray eyes that showed you secrets and mysteries without telling you the answers.

It was difficult keeping his mind on Harry and discipline when she was only a few feet away, her perfume a part of his son, a hint they'd cuddled at one point or another. She'd carried him, Griff guessed. In her arms, cushioned against her softly rounded breasts.

He knew they were rounded. The shirt couldn't hide everything.

He knew they were soft. Everything about her was soft and wonderfully feminine.

He envied his son for having been that close to her.

With an impatient shake of his head, he refocused his thoughts from the sensual to the practical. Harry and his penchant for wandering.

He'd concentrate on Sharron later, when there were no distractions.

"Harry," Griff said, just in case his attention had wandered too.

"Yes, Dad?"

"If you're sorry, then you know it was wrong to come to Sharron's. Right?"

"You didn't say I couldn't come," Harry objected, suddenly looking concerned that he might not be on solid ground here.

"Yes, I did," Griff insisted, trying to remember his exact words.

He didn't have to. Harry remembered for him.

Harry shook his head vehemently. "You said me climbing the wall makes you worry."

Griff nodded. Yeah, he'd said something along those lines.

"So I didn't tell you."

Griff felt his eyebrows climb his forehead. "You thought I wouldn't find out?"

Harry had the grace to look chagrinned. "I didn't think Shawon would call." The toddler shot Sharron a glance that put the blame squarely in her lap.

She pretended not to understand.

Griff sighed heavily, realizing that house rules had to be redefined according to Harry's loophole sense of justice. "I think perhaps we need to talk some more about this, Sport. This is going to take more time than I figured. What do you say we go home and get out of Sharron's way, hmm?"

Harry looked as though he was going to argue, but a warning glance from his father stifled the momentary rebellion. He settled for an expressive sigh, overacted but definitely adorable. Sharron couldn't help but laugh, a lack of judgment which earned her a disgruntled look from Griff.

"Don't encourage him," Griff warned her as they all got to their feet. He told Harry to say good-bye to Sharron.

"Bye, Shawon," Harry said, giving her thighs a quick hug before she had time to bend down.

They were leaving. Caught off guard, although she couldn't imagine why, she just watched as they headed toward the front door. Griff was leaving without another word.

So what did she expect? Harry's dad obviously had more on his mind than following up an unexpected moment of . . . She frowned, not knowing how to finish that. Flirtation? Had it even been that? And was that the end of it?

She hated not knowing.

They were at the door when she remembered the purpose of Harry's visit. "Don't forget your rocket, Harry," she called out, then cringed as he turned and sprinted toward the patio, dodging plants, furniture, and miscellaneous obstacles with careless unconcern. Another visit from Harry would turn her into a basket case if she didn't make some changes in decor.

"I'm sorry about the vase." The closeness of Griff's deep voice startled her, making her jump.

She turned and saw that he hadn't moved from the door. That was odd. She could have sworn he'd been no more than a breath away. Shaking her head in confusion, she said, "The vase wasn't important."

"It's important." Griff leaned back against the door, arms crossed over his chest. "I'm not in the habit of asking for a date in front of my son. I would have called you later."

More than a passing flirtation. She could see it in the way he looked at her. She took a shallow breath. "He cramps your style?"

Griff shook his head. "I don't have a style."

Sharron's gaze swept his clothing before returning to meet his solemn expression, a smile pushing at her mouth. "No argument there."

He looked mildly affronted, but she had to give him credit for not arguing. "That's not what I'm talking about."

"I know."

"Things would have been different if Harry wasn't here now."

"How different?" Her fingers curled into tight fists at her side.

"I'd already know how you taste instead of having to wonder."

Harry dashed back into the room, a toy gripped in each fist, his shoes stuck under his arms. Oh yeah, she remembered. Shoes. Shows what kind of a mom she'd be. She'd been ready to send him home barefoot and hadn't even noticed.

But then, neither had his father.

Griff knelt down to help Harry, stuffing tiny feet into the sneakers and letting Harry do up the Velcro straps. When the shoes were on and both males were standing again, Harry waved and pulled his father out the door.

Before it shut, Griff turned and said, "It'll have to be a few days, Sharron. But don't think I'll forget."

She could hear Harry asking, "Forget what?" as the door closed behind them.

"I like Shawon." Harry's short legs pumped double time to keep up with his father's unhurried stride.

"I like her too," Griff said. And he did, although it was definitely a different kind of liking than Harry's.

"She's alone," Harry said, a pensive look reaching his eyes. "She doesn't want kids."

Griff was surprised, mostly because of how good she'd been with Harry. Gentle and caring, making up with an open heart for what she so obviously lacked in experience.

But she didn't want any of her own. Interesting. "How do you know that?"

"She tol' me. How come she doesn't want any?"

"Did you ask her?" He wasn't surprised when Harry nodded.

"She didn't explain very good."

"I'm not sure I have the answers either, Harry," Griff

said slowly. "Maybe she just doesn't want to get married."

"Don't have to get married to have kids," Harry pointed out. "You didn't."

"That's different, Harry. I didn't want a wife." Running long fingers across Harry's shoulders, he added, "I just wanted you."

"But what if you and Shawon . . ." Harry let the thought trail off into nothing, perhaps not knowing how to end it.

Time to nip that one in the bud, Griff decided. Reaching down to relieve Harry of the toys, he tucked them under one arm and glanced over his shoulder at the two-storied, white-painted home that was Sharron's. It was a big home for a single woman.

He wondered why she chose to live in it alone.

"Don't get any funny ideas, Sport. Remember what I've told you before: I'm not looking for a wife. We've got each other, and that's the way we're going to keep it."

"Yeah, I 'member," Harry mumbled, kicking at a pebble that got in his way.

Griff shot a speculative glance down at his son, noting his drooping shoulders. It couldn't be the subject of marriage that upset him, he knew. Harry loved having his dad to himself; he'd never known it any other way. It was a living arrangement Griff was determined to maintain, more or less. If anything changed, it would be to add a brother or sister for Harry.

Certainly not a wife. He'd made that mistake once already.

"I like Shawon," Harry said, sounding disappointed.

"It's okay to like her as long as you remember she doesn't want to be a mommy."

"I thought *all* girls wanted to be mommies."

"She's a woman, not a girl," Griff said with a private smile.

"There's a difference?"

"Yup." He didn't explain, dwelling instead on what that particular woman would feel like in his arms. She'd be smooth, he knew. Hot and smooth and exciting. His body tightened as he considered a number of different scenarios with the two of them, intimately touching. Discovering how hot was hot.

When a tug from his son kept him from stepping off the curb into the street, Griff realized it was time for a change of subject. "Why do you call her Shawon instead of Sharron?"

Harry grinned up at his father, but declined to respond.

Griff pursued it, curious why his son, who was perfectly capable of pronouncing any word he chose, would suddenly revert to baby talk. He followed Harry up the walk to their house and waited as the child turned the handle with both hands before pushing open the door.

"Come on, Harry. Tell me why you say things like 'sowwy' to her. I know you know better."

Harry turned and looked up at him, his grin a slash of pure delight. "Because she likes it."

FOUR

Harry was nothing if not persistent. Griff tucked the blanket under his son's chin and left the room before Harry could say it again.

I want Shawon.

Soon, he'd told Harry—a thousand times, it seemed. Soon, when he finished the project he was working on.

Not fair. Want to see her now.

Griff walked slowly down the stairs and thought about Harry's demand. He'd read that it was natural for two and three year olds to demand instant gratification for their wants, whether it be ice cream, a hug, or a trip to the playground. He'd read about it, but this was the first time he'd seen the trait in his own son.

Harry wanted to see Sharron, and he wasn't pleased about having to wait.

But then, neither was Griff.

Rubbing a hand across his tired eyes, he wished it was himself he'd just put down for a nap instead of Harry.

Working flat out for three days and nights was beginning to wear on him, and the temptation to turn around and go upstairs to bed was strong. Just a couple of hours, he told himself, and he'd feel better.

A couple of hours' work, though, would see him to the end of the project. Life would become less complicated then, he knew. He'd be able to lie down on the floor beside Harry to watch *Sesame Street*, instead of having to pretend he was watching it from across his drawing table. Without a stack of blueprints to distract him, he'd be able to give Harry a run for his money when they played checkers. And dinner conversation would consist of more than "Use your spoon, not your fingers" or "I want chocolate in my milk."

Griff wished he'd had time to find someone to help him with Harry before he'd become so busy. But then, he hadn't expected to land the account for the new senior citizens home practically the moment they hit town. He'd submitted a proposal for the project before they'd left Chicago, thinking only that it wouldn't hurt to get his name into the arena. He'd won the council's approval, though, and the due date for the preliminary architectural renderings had left him with little choice but to work with Harry underfoot.

And now there was Sharron to consider. Griff paused at the door to his study, shoving his hands into the back pockets of his jeans as he stared at the piles of drawings, blueprints, and coloring books that littered the floor. It had been a long time, he mused, since a woman had interested him enough to make him want to know her better. Over the years since his divorce, he'd managed to keep his dealings with women on one of two levels—amicable or sexual.

With Sharron, he wanted both.

It was about time, he supposed. He'd never seriously imagined he would drift through life without getting involved again. Sharron was the perfect choice . . . if, as Harry had told him, she was sincere about not wanting children. They could have a mutually satisfying relationship without the lies and deceit that were inevitably spawned by a more permanent arrangement.

There was always the chance she wouldn't be interested. Exhaling loudly, Griff picked his way through the rubble toward the other side of the room. Tomorrow, he decided as he slid behind the giant drawing table that was cluttered with the tools of his trade. Tomorrow, he'd put an ad in the paper for someone to watch Harry during the day. Massaging the knot at the base of his neck, Griff took a deep breath and picked up a pencil.

Tomorrow, he'd call Sharron.

Sharron watched as Harry made his way toward her, his feet moving along the wall with more confidence than before. His arms waved energetically as though his balance was threatened, the orange T-shirt he wore above cherry-red shorts a vibrant flag against the green background.

He was definitely getting the hang of it, she mused,

admiring his unhesitating progress. Flailing arms aside, he never missed a step.

Eager for the feel of chubby arms around her neck, she was waiting for him as he neared their established meeting place. It had been three days since Harry had last invaded her garden—three long, lonely days. Vacation blues, she'd told herself. For a person unused to taking more than a handful of days off in a row, all the peace and quiet of her summer vacation was getting to her.

It would be nice to have someone to talk with, even if that someone was breaking rules. Sharron was reminding herself that she wasn't to encourage Harry as he got near enough for her to see the stains on his shirt, evidence of something wet and sticky recently enjoyed. Strangely, her eagerness for a hug was scarcely diminished.

"Hi, Shawon!" Harry's grin was a startling display of blue-stained lips and teeth that invoked all sorts of disgusting images as she tried to imagine what he'd been eating.

"Hi, Harry. What's new?" She leaned against the wall, folding her arms across her chest as she regarded the small boy. The hug would have to wait until she reminded Harry that he wasn't supposed to be there.

"I ate a blue ghost," he said proudly.

She wondered how one removed ectoplasm stains, then decided it wasn't her problem. Harry's dad could tackle that one. "Didn't your dad say you couldn't climb the wall anymore?"

"I'm not climbing. I'm walking."

Yeah, sure. Semantics were a strong justification for

this kid, Sharron thought, fighting back a chuckle. "And you think he'll buy that?"

Harry thought about it for a minute. "Pro'bly not. You gonna call him?"

"I gotta do it, Harry. He needs to know where you are." Sharron held her arms open then, giving only the barest thought to how her pink top would look with blue ghost stains on it. Thinking she'd check ectoplasm in the handy-dandy book of stains she'd received for Christmas, she missed the mischievous gleam in Harry's eyes.

The only warning she had was his battle cry. "Cowabunga!" he yelled, and launched himself off the wall, throwing all thirty-odd pounds into her outstretched arms.

"Harry!" she yelled, urging caution when it was already too late. His arms looped around her neck, and Sharron grabbed what she could of him as she fought for balance. She backstepped, sidestepped, and backstepped again, not caring where she put her feet as long as she managed to stay on them. It was a lost cause, though. The ground was too uneven, too squishy for such fancy footwork.

She finally lost it, only just managing to fall backward so she wouldn't crush Harry. Not that he was aware of the potential for harm. No, Harry bounced against her tummy and screeched into her shoulder, his delight as unequivocal as his lack of fear.

The ground was soft under her back, the spongy soil a fortunate by-product of her diligent tending over the last few days, the flowers an uneven pillow. Soft, she repeated gratefully. With luck, the only bruises she'd get were from where Harry's knees were grinding into her hips.

"Whoops!" He giggled against the side of her neck, then pushed his fists into her shoulders in an attempt to sit up.

Lifting her head from a pillow of heavily scented gardenias, Sharron focused on the laughing child. "Whoops?" she repeated. "You knock me off my feet, destroy my garden, and all you can say is 'whoops'?"

"Sowwy?" he tried, but his giggles overcame his sincerity.

It was hopeless. How could she resist the mischievous light that danced in his eyes? Why should she even want to? Putting aside for the moment the facts that her back was coated in mud and fertilizer and her head was crushing her prized gardenias—not to mention what her fanny was doing to whatever she'd landed on there—did she have anything better to do on a hot summer afternoon?

Not really.

Harry kind of gurgled, then screamed delightedly when her fingers found the sensitive spots on his sides. Rolling off her tummy and onto a previously undamaged group of flowers, he commenced his own attack. Pudgy fingers dug into Sharron's sides, smearing mud where she'd been clean. She laughed more at this determination than his accuracy, rising to her knees as her longer arms outwitted and outmaneuvered the small boy.

It was a mud-slinging, no-holds-barred free-for-all.

By the time Sharron called a halt to the fracas, more than one posie had been smashed beyond any hope of revival. Dragging a reluctant Harry over to the patio, she tugged off his clothes and shoes, then turned the hose on him. Screeches of protest at the icy shower soon evolved into screams of glee. Harry pranced under the cold water in the warm afternoon sunshine until Sharron was satisfied the mud was going to stay outside. Slipping out of her own shoes, she sluiced the mud from her arms and legs, shivering as the cold water got off track and coursed down her spine, saturating her clothes. With the pockets and cuffs of her shorts still filled with mud, she lost her tolerance for cold water. She reached down to turn off the spigot, then hefted a goose-bump covered Harry onto her hip.

"Let's get you warmed up, Harry." Knowing she was leaving a trail but incapable of finding another way to get from point *A* to point *B*, she tiptoed through the living room and down the long hallway that led to her bedroom and bath. She set Harry down on the thick rug in front of the tub.

"Frozen." Harry's teeth chattered pitifully as she pulled a towel from the linen closet and knelt to rub him down. She worked him over good, not satisfied until the goose bumps had all disappeared. Grabbing a dry towel, she wrapped it around Harry.

"Warm?" she asked.

He nodded, then sneezed right in her face.

"Achoo to you too," she retorted, dragging a corner of the towel over her face. "Sure hope you're not catching cold, Harry."

"'Scuze me," he said, and just as she was reaching for

a tissue for him, he sneezed again. She held the tissue to his nose, wiping her face again with the towel.

"Okay now?" she asked, looking forward to her own shower for more reasons than one.

"Okay." Harry sniffled and sank back into the towel.

"Good. We need to call your dad." She ignored the lower lip that thrust out at her words and pulled him over to the phone by her bed. She punched out the numbers as Harry called them off, then handed him the phone, conscious for the first time that her own skin was covered in thousands of goose bumps and that she was dripping muddy water all over the carpet. Terrific. She wondered if Griff was as good at cleaning carpet as he was at sweeping.

Harry kept it short. "Hi, Dad." There was a short pause, then he said, "Shawon's." Another pause, a silent nod, and "'Bye."

So much for your basic call home, she thought as she went into the bathroom to get another dry towel for Harry. She settled him in the center of her bed, making sure he was covered nose to toe. "I need to get in the shower, kiddo. Think you can stay out of trouble for five minutes?"

"Shore." He snuggled deeper into the towels.

Shore? She could only hope it meant what she thought it did. "Don't move from the bed unless your dad comes. Then you can let him in." She headed toward the bathroom.

"I'm not allowed to answer the door."

Sharron paused midstride. "This is special," she said carefully. "We both know it will be your dad."

"What if it isn't?"

She could feel the mud from her shorts oozing down her legs. "Yell through the door, Harry. If he answers, go ahead and open it."

"What if I can't reach . . . ?"

At this rate, Griffin Ross would be there before she got into the shower. "So he'll just have to wait." She fled into the bathroom.

Sharron stepped into the shower fully clothed, wincing under the cold spray that ever so slowly turned to warm. She stripped, dropping the muddy garments onto the tiled floor at her feet. By the time her panties and bra had joined the shorts and shirt, the water was warm enough to make her wish she had time to enjoy it. She didn't. Griff was going to be there any second, and Harry probably couldn't reach the knob on the front door. Ducking her head under the stream of water, she rinsed the dirt from her hair as she whipped a bar of soap over her limbs. Leaving her clothes in a wet, muddy pile, she shut off the spray and stepped out onto the rug. She hurriedly whipped a thick bath sheet around her still-wet body, tucking the end between her breasts before wrapping another around her head.

Pushing open the door to the bedroom, she flashed a smile toward Harry on her way to the dresser. The sight of Griff sprawled beside his son—*on her bed!*—sent her heartbeat into a mad race with her scrambling thoughts. She came to an abrupt standstill, not quite stumbling, but not a graceful halt either.

It was one of those silences that lasted an eternity.

Sharron stared at Griff, who stared right back at her, his smile challenging Harry's for innocence.

He never moved, yet she felt his growing nearness with every sense she possessed. She knew he saw all of her, yet his gaze never dropped below her nose. *All of her*— even though the towel left only her lower legs and arms exposed. Her shoulders, too, but not much else. Hardly a risqué revelation, she thought with surprising lucidity, yet she was left feeling she'd revealed an intimate side of her that no man had ever seen.

Her heart did a curious thing then. The uneven, racing beat slowed, and she could feel her pulse begin to normalize. The beat was still much faster than usual, but it was almost as though the tempo was in familiar, *previously learned* territory.

Where she belonged.

For a moment, it seemed her heart stopped altogether, only to resume beating at that same, now familiar rhythm.

Where had she learned it?

Griff's slow, easy smile made her clutch at the towel and wonder if he saw more than she imagined. More than she was prepared to share with him.

More than she could afford to lose.

Harry wiggled his way out of his towel and threw his arms around Griff's neck. "Dad's here."

"I noticed." She'd noticed.

"Hello, Sharron. Nice to see you." Gently unlocking Harry's fingers, he sat up on the bed—her bed—all the while fending off his son's playful attack.

Sharron cleared her throat. "What are you doing here?"

Griff looked surprised. "You called me."

"I meant my bedroom." Her fingers curled into the towel. "What are you doing in here?"

"Harry was determined to do as he was told—for a change—so I decided I'd better keep him company." He caught Harry's chin between his fingers and stared resolutely into his eyes. "Speaking of which, it would be nice if you minded me as well as you do Sharron. I thought I told you no more climbing the wall."

"I wasn't climbing. I was walking." Harry grabbed his towel, which had fallen by the wayside, and pulled it around his head, effectively hiding his expression.

Griff sighed and opened a flap of the towel in the vicinity of Harry's ear. "We'll talk when we get home, Sport."

"Shore, Dad," Harry mumbled from his cocoon.

Griff's attention switched back to Sharron. "Harry tells me you were rolling in the mud. Wish you'd invited me. I could have used a break." His slow drawl brought the goose bumps back.

"It was a spur of the moment thing." Her toes dug into the carpet as his gaze slid across her shoulders to where she clutched the towel at her breasts. "Don't you suppose you should wait outside while I change?"

Griff slid off the bed and crossed to her. "It never occurred to me that you'd panic to find me here."

"I'm not panicked."

His laugh disagreed with her. "So why are your

knuckles white?" he asked, his gaze caressing her clenched fingers at her breast, then rising slowly to reveal a stark, undisguised desire that couldn't be mistaken for anything else.

A hunger such as none she'd ever experienced built deep inside of her, the essence of that sensitivity beginning at her feminine core and flaring outward. She gasped softly and wondered if it was her turn to speak because, for the life of her, she couldn't remember what they were talking about.

Harry saved her. "Can I go watch TV?"

"May I," she said, her eyes never leaving Griff.

"You can come, too, Shawon, but I'm going to watch *Beetle Juice* and I bet you won't like it."

"That's not what I—"

Griff interrupted. "Go on, Harry. I'll be there in a minute."

"Don't break anything," Sharron felt compelled to say.

"Don't touch anything," Griff added as Harry cleared the door, the long towel trailing in his wake. Griff reached out and pushed the door closed behind him.

Sharron pretended that the sound of the door clicking shut didn't strain her already rattled sensibilities. "I thought 'don't break anything' was explicit enough."

He shook his head. "'Don't break anything' means he can still touch. It is therefore an accident when something actually gets broken. 'Don't touch' means exactly that."

"Did you have to go to a special school to learn how to talk to kids?"

"You pick it up as you go along." He gave a long sigh, his warm breath gliding across her shoulders. "You'll notice I'm still learning with Harry. I should have been more attuned to the difference between climbing and walking. He's going to break something if he ever falls from that wall."

"Actually, he seems to have a terrific sense of balance. I don't think you need to worry about him falling."

"He gets that from me. I wanted to be a tightrope walker when I was his age."

"But I thought he was adopted . . ." His teasing grin made her shake her head in exasperation. "Cute, Griff. I suppose you're going to try to tell me he inherited your charm too."

"Nature versus nurture," he murmured. "You never know what's going to rub off on a kid."

He was so close now, she had to tilt her head back, an adjustment that unbalanced the towel on her head. She made a grab for it a moment too late, just as it unwound and fell from her hair. The long, damp strands tumbled down her back, making her shiver.

Any excuse in a pinch, Griff thought.

He touched his finger to a long strand that curled along her shoulder. The curl straightened, then wound around his finger as though attracted to something male. He smiled and tucked the strand behind her ear, then draw his finger across the bridge of her nose and down to her chin. "Your skin is soft, like satin. Will you have dinner with me tomorrow?"

"Tomorrow?"

"Hmm, tomorrow. You're still wet, you know," he murmured, catching a drop of moisture from her chin with his finger and bringing it to his lips. "Want some help drying off?"

A strangled noise was all he got for an answer. He laughed, then said, "Perhaps not. Anyway, Harry needs a change of clothes. What about tomorrow, Sharron?"

"I'm sure I'll be dry by then."

He laughed again. "I was talking about dinner, honey."

The dialogue and the attraction between them were leaping recklessly in asides, forwards, and assumptions. Sharron was breathless from the pace. "You said you'd call."

"I like this better." He brushed his knuckles across hers where she clutched the towel. "Don't you?"

Her knuckles burned, the fire licking at them with a provocation that was there, then suddenly gone as his hand fell away. She stared up at him, so close that his unshaven face nearly touched hers. She wondered how it would feel, the brush of his chin across her bare shoulders. . . .

"What do you say, Sharron? Will you have dinner with me?" His words were a low rumble that barely reached her ears.

Suddenly, she felt wildly daring. "Are you going to shave?"

It was back, that deliberately hungry gaze that made her blood pulse hot and fast. Her tongue darted out to stroke lips that were dry, the moist tip gliding across and over as he watched. Her lips stayed parted, and her breath came in shallow spurts as she waited . . . waited for him to end the suspense.

His thumb was suddenly riding the swell of her lower lip, long fingers cupping the side of her face. She trembled, shattered by the small caress, then trembled all over again as he bent to rub his cheek across hers.

A moment, that was all, and when he lifted his head, she could only think that she wanted more.

His voice was a low growl. "I'd better shave, honey. Your skin is too sensitive, and I might not remember to be careful with you."

She took a deep breath to control the heated response fueled by his words, yet couldn't help the teasing smile that came to her lips. "I'll come anyway."

A surprised laugh erupted from his chest. "You're not exactly shy, are you?"

"Usually I am."

"But not with me."

He was confident, almost arrogantly so. It gave her a feeling so feminine . . . so compellingly exciting . . . that she was incapable of arguing. "Not with you," she said quietly.

With a final pass of his thumb across her lips, he dropped his hand from her face. His eyes were dark and clouded with desire. "Good. It'll be simpler that way."

"What will be simpler?"

He gave her a long look that was mildly chiding, then continued as though she hadn't spoken. "You're shy, but not with me. Tell me, Sharron. Will you also be bold, but only with me?"

She twisted the towel tighter. "How would I know? I hardly know you."

"But you've admitted you're not shy with me."

"I lied."

"That remains to be seen." The corners of his mouth tipped in a slight smile at her audible gasp. "Don't lose your nerve now, honey. Not when it's getting interesting."

"I've never—"

He finished for her. "Never flirted with a man you hardly know . . . in the privacy of your bedroom . . . wearing nothing more than a towel?"

She swallowed. "I guess that about covers it."

"Don't worry about it, honey. I like the idea that you're more innocent than experienced."

"I didn't say I was innocent."

"Maybe not in so many words, Sharron, but your responses speak volumes." He lifted a hand to cup her face. "I can't remember knowing a woman who was so totally honest about what she felt. Didn't anyone ever teach you to hold a little something back?"

"I haven't had all that many . . . teachers," she said hesitantly. "Life's been hectic enough without those kinds of complications."

"So what in your life has changed?" His fingers tunneled through the wet hair above her ear, lightly massaging her scalp as she tried to think of an answer that wouldn't reveal how little she knew about the opposite sex. Her one brief affair during college hadn't prepared her for Griff.

But then, she wondered, how could anyone have prepared her for the man who sent her heart racing with only a look?

"What makes you think anything has changed?" she finally asked.

"Because if you've ever looked at another man the way you look at me, we wouldn't be talking about your innocence."

"I told you, Griff. I'm not exactly—"

His fingers covered her lips. "Don't worry about it, honey. I think I like the idea of teaching you."

Her bottom lip quivered under his touch. "I shouldn't get involved with you," she said softly.

"Why not?"

"What if it leads to something?" She was deliberately vague, yet knowing it had to be said. "I've never wanted to have children. You already have one."

"Not to worry. I don't want a wife."

The bluntness of his reply slammed into her heart. He smiled as he gently traced the curve of her lips. "So you see, Sharron, we've got nothing to worry about. In fact, I'd say we're perfect for each other."

"Why?"

"Because neither of us will be disappointed."

Suddenly, his fingers were gone and he'd moved to open the bedroom door. He was halfway out the door before he looked back over his shoulder. "I don't suppose you know any baby-sitters, do you?"

She shook her head. Of course she didn't. Nor did she have a clue as to how one went about finding one. Parenting was certainly full of challenges, she thought, wishing she could be more help. Unfortunately, she was the last person who was capable of doing just that. With surprise, she realized she was somewhat disappointed in herself.

Griff just shrugged. "Never mind, I'll figure something out. Unless you hear from me, plan on leaving about seven."

"Seven," she repeated, the fingers of both hands curling around the towel. Dinner with Griff. Summer vacation was definitely looking up.

"I'll bring the towel Harry's wearing back then. If you'll stick his wet clothes in a bag . . ."

"I can manage that. But his shoes—"

"He's got more. Just throw them in with the clothes." He gave her a crooked smile. "Thanks for cleaning him up. Sorry if he was a bother. He was supposed to be sleeping. Must have slipped out while I was working."

"No bother. My flowers may never get over it, but I had fun."

"So did Harry." Griff's eyes twinkled a teasing dare. "He said you started it."

"I'll get him for that," she promised, fully aware she was looking forward to it.

"I'll be sure to warn him—right after I finish redefining the house rules about leaving the property."

"What is a blue ghost?"

"A Popsicle. Why?"

"Nothing. Just something he said." Not only had Harry snuck out of the house, he'd raided the freezer en route. Sharron couldn't bring herself to tattle on him, figuring he was in enough trouble already. Besides, the evidence on his hands and face had been washed away with the hose. She made a decision to wash his clothes, too, before returning them.

Her allegiance was slanting firmly toward the younger male in the Ross family. Kind of.

Griff shook his head in amused disbelief, but didn't pursue it as he edged out the door. Just when she thought he was going to pull it closed behind him, he turned and narrowed his gaze on her mouth. "I'm going to spend the time between now and tomorrow night fantasizing that you'll wear something that matches your lips."

She gulped as the blood rushed to her face, bemused by Griff's ability to shift between the practical and the erotic. "My lips?" was all she managed to respond.

He nodded just once, his eyes lifting to meet hers. "They're such a beautiful, lush red. Do you know your mouth always looks like it's just been kissed?"

"Um . . ."

He didn't wait for her response. "Maybe something strapless, with your hair up so that your shoulders are bare. The only thing touching them would be the moonlight . . . and me." He cocked an ear toward the living room and gave her a half smile that was filled with regret. "Tomorrow, honey. And try to remember you're not shy. Not with me."

He pulled the door closed with a quiet click, leaving before she could reply to his outrageous challenge. A dress to match her lips. Strapless. *Bare shoulders!* She stared at the closed door and wondered how on earth she'd ever get up the nerve to do as he asked.

"Not shy," she said to no one in particular. "Now whatever gave him that idea?"

FIVE

"Chicken pox? You're kidding!" Sharron pressed the phone to her ear in disbelief.

"It's kind of hard to misdiagnose," Griff said dryly. "Rash, spots, blisters—the whole works."

"But he was fine yesterday."

"The rash started around dinnertime. By the time I got through to his pediatrician this morning, he was already getting a few blisters."

"Poor Harry," she murmured. "I'll bet he's perfectly miserable."

Griff gave a short bark of a laugh. "Poor Harry, nothing! I'm spending all my time entertaining him and fixing his favorite foods. He's having the time of his life."

"How's that? I thought he was sick."

"Technically, yes. But like a lot of kids his age who get chicken pox, he's only got minor symptoms. No fever, no headaches, just a mad craving to scratch every square inch of his body." There was a pause during which she could have sworn she heard the tail end of a badly muffled yawn. "He's up and tearing all over the place. Except for having trouble sleeping last night because of the itching, he's in primo condition."

"It doesn't sound like Harry's the only one who didn't get any sleep last night," she said, homing in on the cause of the yawn.

He snorted. "It's my job to try to keep him from scratching. That doesn't leave a lot of time for much else."

"Is this a roundabout way of telling me dinner's off?"

"That's up to you. I can't leave Harry, though, so we'd have to eat here. Have you ever had chicken pox?"

Her brow furrowed in thought. "I'm not sure. I'd have to check."

"You probably have," he said, yawning again. "Very few kids make it through childhood without getting it."

"How did Harry manage to catch it? Do you know?"

"Incubation is twelve to sixteen days, or about the time we were in Oregon for a long weekend. I'd say he picked it up from one of the kids he played with there."

"Exactly how contagious is it?"

"Very. Harry's under house quarantine for the duration."

"I'll check and let you know."

"We should probably wait a day or two anyway. At the moment, it's all I can do to keep up with Harry."

"That's okay. I've got some leftovers I've been meaning to get to." She opened the refrigerator, cradling the phone between shoulder and ear as she searched for something that would make her boast a fact. There wasn't anything, of course. She slammed the door in disgust and leaned back against it. Pizza again. "In the meantime, Griff, is there anything I can leave on your doorstep or whatever?"

"Thanks, but one of the mom's already offered to go to the store for me."

She straightened from the refrigerator. "One of what moms? I thought you were in quarantine."

He gave his first real laugh of the afternoon. "It depends on your point of view. Did you know how efficiently the rumor mill in this town operates? I only called the doc and the pharmacist, and it's all over town now that Harry has chicken pox. The phone's been ringing non-stop with moms asking if their children can come play with him."

"Kids who've already had chicken pox?" That made sense, particularly if Harry was bored from playing alone. Keeping him occupied was going to be a challenge if he couldn't get out and about. That's what small towns were all about, she told herself, a warm spot building somewhere near her heart. Everyone pitching in to help out with a sick kid.

She loved this town.

"Nope," Griff answered. "These are kids who *haven't* had it yet. They'll take turns coming to play with Harry over the next few days."

She held the phone at arm's length and stared at it in patent disbelief before bringing it back to her ear. "You're not serious?"

"Look at it this way, Sharron. There's no vaccination against chicken pox, so most kids get it eventually. If they get it in the summer, there's no school to miss."

Sharron couldn't believe what she was hearing. "So the moms want to expose their kids to it now because it's *convenient?*"

The television suddenly blared in the background, and Griff took a second to shout at Harry to turn it down. "There's that. And then there's also the argument that the older you get, the harder it hits. Adults can be absolutely miserable while someone as young as Harry just about skates through it."

"This is bizarre. There must be a law against it."

"Uh-uh. And as long as Harry's feeling so well, it makes a lot of sense."

It sounded positively absurd to Sharron, but what did she know? She hadn't been to that school that taught parents all the preposterous rules required for raising children. "So by breathing the same air, these kids might end up with chicken pox?"

A strangling noise reached her ears. "Actually, it's something to do with the nose and throat. You know how kids are, forever chewing on a toy that was just in another kid's mouth. Or sneezing all over the place. Or—"

"That's revolting!" she interrupted, cutting off the graphic description before she gagged. "Is that how you deliberately expose kids? Have Harry sneeze all over them?"

He laughed. "Nothing that disgusting. We'll just let them play, not get upset when they drink from the same glass, maybe have them share a cookie."

She gagged. "I'm going to be sick."

"Which is why you shouldn't come over, not for a couple of days anyway." His voice lowered a notch. "Sorry I didn't call earlier, Sharron. It's been a zoo over here."

"An asylum is more like it," she muttered.

He ignored the commentary. "Tell me, honey, were you going to wear the dress?"

"What dress?" As if she didn't perfectly well know. She'd spent all morning shopping for it, had had to go all the way into San Francisco before finding exactly what she wanted—a strapless, full-skirted confection of scarlet silk that made her feel feminine, sexy, and incredibly shy all at once.

She really needed to get over the shy part. Griff wasn't expecting it. Not, she reminded herself with a grimace, that he was expecting to see her at all. Perhaps it was just as well. She'd been so ridiculously keyed up since the day before that it would have been a minor miracle if she'd actually managed to wear Griff's scarlet fantasy.

Bold, he'd said. She just didn't think she had it in her.

His sigh broke into her thoughts. "I've had a rotten twenty-four hours, Sharron. The fantasy of eventually seeing you in a sexy dress is about all that's keeping me going."

"Oh. That dress." She swallowed hard and waited.

His chuckle was a deep, husky rumble that was almost a physical rub on her senses. "Yeah. That dress."

Her tongue stuck to the top of her mouth as she

frantically searched for something to say. It was still stuck when Griff ended the silence.

"I'll call you later tonight, Sharron. Harry wants to talk with you now." He passed the phone to Harry without giving her a chance to say good-bye.

"Hi, Shawon. I got the pox."

She giggled, assuming Harry couldn't possibly know pox was slang for syphilis. All the same, she hoped his dad might provide some guidance in using the full word. "Chicken pox doesn't sound like a lot of fun, kiddo. Is your dad playing a lot of games with you?"

"Mmm. My favorite is hide-and-seek, but you know what?"

"What?"

He lowered his voice to a whisper. "He's not very good at it. I find him real easy every time."

She bit off another giggle. "Maybe you should give him extra time to find a good place to hide."

"I can't count to a hundred," he mumbled, "and that's how long he pro'bly needs."

"Pro'bly." She gave it a couple of seconds' thought. "Why don't you count to ten five times."

"Is that a hundred?"

"It's fifty."

There was a short pause. "How many times do I have to count to ten to make a hundred?"

"Ten."

"I can do that!" He sounded remarkably more cheerful. "Thanks, Shawon. You're awfully smart."

"Thanks, Harry." A lump developed in her throat from out of nowhere.

"Have you had the pox, Shawon?"

She swallowed over yet another giggle until there were tears in her eyes. "I'm not sure, Harry. I'll look it up and let you know when I talk to you next."

"If not, I can give it to you," he said earnestly.

"I think I'm too old to want it," she replied. "Tell you what, though. I'll come visit you if I find out I've already had it."

"Okay, Shawon." In the distance, she could hear the ring of the doorbell. "I gotta go now and give some kids the pox. 'Bye."

He hung up before she could tell him that, just perhaps, he might want to call it something else.

"He's wearing the jammies that have feet sewn in," Griff told Sharron over the phone. "And I put his bib overalls on top so he couldn't pull down the zipper and scratch his stomach. The only thing he can possibly reach to scratch is his face, and he hasn't got a rash or any blisters there yet."

"It's July, Griff. Harry's going to have heatstroke under all those clothes." Sharron rolled onto her side, kicking free of the sheet that was tangled around her feet. The luminous dial on the clock showed half past eleven. She'd been lying in bed, waiting for him to call.

It had never occurred to her that he wouldn't.

"He'll be okay. I put a fan in his room."

His voice was an intimate murmur, filling her with all sorts of erotic images without having strayed from the topic of his son. She fought to maintain a sense of balance under its husky caress. "How many batches of kids did Harry go through today?"

"Two. I think he's got at least a dozen more showing up tomorrow to submit to the pox."

She laughed. "You really shouldn't encourage him, Griff. I can only imagine what the moms had to say."

"You don't want to know," she heard him mutter. "So tell me, Sharron. Have you had it?"

"Afraid not. I double-checked with my mom just to be sure." A breeze wafted in through the open terrace door, gently buffeting the sheer silk gown she wore. She smiled to herself, exquisitely aware of the sensual feel of the silk against her skin.

All because of the man at the other end of the phone. His voice was doing crazy things to her senses.

"Too bad." Griff reached across to his nightstand and flicked off the light before settling back against the pillows. The sheets were cool against his naked skin, but he knew they wouldn't stay that way long. His body was already warming at the sound of her voice.

He could listen to her forever.

She obliged his unspoken request and continued. "It's probably because I wasn't around other kids much. At the time, though, Mom considered me lucky not to get every cold and other disease that was going around."

"No brothers or sisters?" he asked.

"Nary a one." She laughed, remembering the look on

her parents' faces when she'd turned six and demanded a sibling. "They told me they felt blessed to get a healthy, bright, and cute child on the first try, and didn't want to take the chance they'd muck it up on a second go-round."

"You believed them?"

"Not even a smidge. After going through the terrible twos and ferocious fours with me, they were probably too exhausted to start all over."

"You were a handful?" he asked, chuckling as he tried to picture Sharron as anything less than a perfect, compliant child. He couldn't.

She almost told him that the vague memories she had of those early years, of her loneliness, the pressure to fulfill the hopes of her parents and teachers, were half the reason she didn't want any children of her own. She didn't, though, saying instead, "Fortunately for them— and me, I suppose—I grew out of that stage before they reached the end of their patience."

"So what were you doing that you weren't around other kids—besides driving your folks crazy?"

"Practicing, mostly." She paused, and he could hear the rustling of linens as she snuggled deeper into the pillows. He wondered what she was wearing. Her voice was deeper when she spoke again, softer. "From fifth grade onward, I had tutors instead of having to go to school. I guess it makes sense I've missed getting chicken pox."

"The piano?" he asked, revising his previous assumption that her playing was a hobby.

"Mm-hmm."

"Tell me more." He closed his eyes, following the story as she told him about the years of training. The conservatory where she lived, breathed, and slept until her early twenties. Then the concert circuit and her life as a performer.

A life which she'd decided to abandon in favor of settling down. "I woke up on my twenty-ninth birthday and decided I hated all the traveling. My parents went into shock when I told them I was going to teach music at the university."

"Where are your parents now?"

"Charleston. When they're not gnashing their teeth about my decision, they run a music store that keeps the city's budding musicians supplied with instruments and the like."

"So it runs in the family. How did you end up in Wagner?" he asked, shifting uncomfortably onto his side as the sheets warmed against his back. "The nearest university is down near San Francisco."

"Which is just an hour or less. Not much of a commute, especially if I manage my hours to avoid traffic. I also don't plan on being there more than three or four days a week." She stretched her arms high above her head, then curled back around the phone. "Besides, I already had the house here."

"Since when?"

"About eight years, but I've lived here more off than on. I bought the house when I was just beginning to make money." She paused, then said, "I needed somewhere to come home to in between tours. It gave me a sense of balance to know I could come home and unpack in a room that was mine."

His mind drew a picture of Sharron as he was beginning to know her . . . as she must have been before giving it all up. Dressed in something long and flowing, her hair tucked up in a sophisticated knot, her hands bare of jewelry—her classical beauty a circumstance of nature. She was seated before an enormous concert grand piano, the stage illuminated with brilliant lights, a full orchestra filling in behind her.

The music, he knew, would be extraordinary, reaching to the edges of emotion and beyond. Because Sharron was an extraordinarily emotional woman. Kind, as she was with Harry. Playful. Frightened yet composed, another trait she'd demonstrated with Harry. Caring.

And sexy. Sensual. She'd shown him a dozen sides of herself, and they'd only just begun. It was a good thing she didn't want kids, he mused, or he'd be in trouble.

He took a deep, calming breath and asked for more. "Won't you miss performing?"

"Not really. The university has me signed up for a few concerts over the next year or so. That should be enough to satisfy the exhibitionist side of my nature." She paused, then said, "Your turn, Griffen Ross. What does Harry's dad do with his days?"

He chuckled. "Lately, it seems that raising Harry is all I've got time for."

"Have you given any thought to daycare?"

"Um-hmm. But I can't seem to get the time to do anything about it." He explained about the senior citizens home—for which he'd finished the preliminary renderings—and the new bank at the north end of town—which he hadn't.

"An architect," she said after he'd outlined the basics. "I never would have guessed."

"What did you think?"

There was a moment's hesitation before she replied. "I don't know. I guess I never thought much beyond you being Harry's father."

"Now I know why moms who don't work outside the home are so touchy about it," he muttered. "Do you have any idea how much time kids take?"

"I'm beginning to." She laughed lightly, then sighed. "Where were you, before coming to Wagner?"

"Chicago. I decided I wanted Harry to grow up near the ocean, so we came here."

"Wagner is a fifteen-minute drive from the water," she pointed out.

"Close enough. I plan to build a house on the cliffs when I find the right lot."

So he wouldn't be living at the other end of the garden wall forever. Sharron bit back a sigh of regret, then chided herself for minding. After all, it wasn't as though there was a possibility of anything permanent between them. A flirtation, yes. Anything more, well, they'd just have to see.

But forever? Definitely not.

Irritated for a reason she didn't understand, she made a pretense of being too sleepy to talk anymore, said good-bye, and hung up the phone before he could argue.

For a long time afterward, she stared into the shadows of the night and wondered at the wisdom of getting involved, at any level, with a man who had a son named Harry.

It was raining outside when Griff called Sharron the next evening. He didn't ask why she'd hung up so quickly the night before. Instead, he picked up where they had left off, digging into the facts of her world, sharing his. Harry was a mass of blisters, he said, and thanked her for the new coloring book and crayons she'd left on the doorstep.

No big deal, she told him, settling easily into the rhythm of his questions and answers as though a full day hadn't passed. The irritation—at herself, she'd realized—had faded. In its place was an understanding of what was happening between them.

They were attracted to each other, and they were probably going to act on that attraction. Even her relative inexperience with men didn't keep her from realizing the facts. Harry, she'd decided, was part of the equation only in that he lived with his father.

Nothing to do with her at all.

Calmed by the facts, Sharron opened herself to what turned out to be a nightly session of laughter and sighs—laughter because they sincerely enjoyed talking together, sighs because it would have been even better if they didn't have to do it on the phone. They talked about everything and then some, discovering likes and dislikes, and skimming the surface of more serious issues because such things were meant to be discussed face-to-face.

Things like why he never wanted to marry.

Things like why she didn't want to have children.

She admitted to a growing curiosity as to why he was adamant about not giving Harry a mother, but he put off her tentative questions for another time. Put off, but promised her an answer.

Just as she promised to explain why she didn't want children.

A week later, she felt as though she knew him better than she'd known anyone in her life.

A week later, he asked her to come for dinner . . . because it was time. He'd cook for her, if she didn't mind steak and salad. He really didn't want to leave Harry with a sitter, not when he was still borderline sick.

And she needn't worry. Harry was no longer contagious.

The pox had run its course.

SIX

Griff and Harry's home was on the other side of the block and down a ways, just far enough that she was beginning to doubt the wisdom of wearing high-heeled sandals. It would have been much smarter to wear sneakers, as she had the handful of times the past week when she'd cruised by to drop off care packages that more often than not included more calamine lotion for Harry, not to mention the clothes she'd managed to free of blue-ghost stains.

Sneakers, though, would have scaled down her outfit from the casually chic to casually casual, and that had been enough incentive to leave them on the floor of her closet.

The house came into view not a moment too soon, her feet beginning to protest at the rough demands of heels and hiking. It was a modern redwood-and-glass dwelling that was all angles and light, and flanked on either side by a pair of rather stuffy-looking, traditional homes. She followed the flagstone path that cut across the front lawn, the fingers of one hand smoothing the full skirt of the tropical-patterned dress she'd finally chosen. It wasn't the color of her lips, and the thin straps that held up the loose bodice weren't according to specifications either.

The dress was cotton, too, not silk. Cotton was a sensible choice because silk wouldn't take a greasy spill as a joke . . . and wasn't there always the threat of disaster when dining with a toddler? Sharron assumed so. At least, that was the excuse she'd rehearsed for the past hour. Taking a deep breath, she mounted the steps and looked for the doorbell. Not finding it, she rapped her knuckles against the door before she lost her nerve.

Perhaps he wouldn't even notice what she was wearing.

He noticed. Griff answered her knock so quickly, she all but fell through the threshold. His hands shot out and caught her by the upper arms, holding her steady as his eyes did a quick, thorough study of her. From the loose curls that half covered her back and shoulders down to her red-painted toenails, he missed nothing.

Finally, his gaze found hers. "Chicken out?"

It was impossible to lie to those soft, laughing eyes. "I chickened out. You're disappointed?"

"How could I be disappointed? You look fabulous."

"So do you," she murmured before she could stop herself. She no longer held it against him that he'd wanted to shave. If possible, his face was even more interesting sans beard, the strong, sharp planes appealing without being too handsome. She was wondering which she preferred, when it occurred to her he wasn't dressed in one of the bizarre, uncoordinated outfits she'd become accustomed to seeing him in. A long-sleeved pink shirt with the cuffs rolled up to his elbows was tucked into beige slacks. Her study ended at his feet which were bare inside brown Top-Siders.

Her gaze slid upward to meet his. "And here I thought you were color-blind."

His eyes clouded in confusion, then suddenly cleared. "Harry's going through a phase of wanting to pick out what we wear."

"Harry's color-blind?"

Griff laughed and shook his head. "I think he's just being creative. Besides which, he gets a kick out of making me look like a neon sign."

"So where was he when you got dressed tonight?"

"You approve?" he asked softly, his hands rubbing her arms as they stood in the doorway and stared into each other's smile.

"I approve."

"Then I'm glad I took the trouble to divert him with a new picture book while I dressed." He gave her arms another squeeze, then snagged her wrist and pulled her into the house. He led her through a spacious living room and straight into the kitchen. "We can talk in here without waking Harry."

"He's in bed?"

"Of course he's in bed. It's after seven o'clock. Thanks for not ringing the bell, though. It's touch and go for the first few minutes after I put him down."

She took credit where none was due, remaining silent as Griff lifted her onto a kitchen stool. He moved on to the refrigerator to pull out a bottle of wine. At her nod, he poured her a glass and one for himself before taking his place on the other side of the counter, where preparations for dinner were in progress. He picked up a head of lettuce from the sink and began tearing off the leaves.

The speed with which they'd come from door to kitchen left her feeling vaguely disoriented. But then, being around Griff always left her feeling much the same way. His hands on her arms, her wrist, at her waist . . . So easily did he set the fire inside of her that it took all the stage presence she'd learned and rehearsed to keep it a secret.

Secret, ha! Sharron suspected there was very little he didn't know about her reactions to him. The casually predatory way that he was looking at her from across the counter told her that much. She deliberately ignored his gaze and looked around the kitchen, surprised to discover how large and well equipped it was. Copper pans hung from hooks above the center island, and gleaming appliances that appeared larger than normal were scattered around the room. The cooktop was unlike any she'd seen outside of a commercial kitchen, six gas burners rather than the usual four. The refrigerator was oversize, too, and there were three ovens. No—make that four, she corrected, spotting another beneath the counter. Added to scads of counter space with built-in chopping blocks and marble slabs, it was a kitchen designed for a cook. A great cook.

Obviously, throwing steaks on the grill would be a snap for Griff.

"Why do I get the impression I'll get a better meal here than anywhere else in Wagner?" she asked, mesmerized by the movements of his long fingers as they tore at the lettuce.

"The kitchen, you mean?"

"Um-hmm. It makes mine look like the galley on a fifteen-foot sloop."

He grinned. "The people who owned the house before me entertained a lot. With me, cooking is just a hobby. I have to admit, though, it's nice to have a kitchen big enough so that Harry can be in here and I don't trip over him."

"You could have a baseball team in here and not notice."

"I expect that will be the case one of these days. Harry's already talking about T-ball, but I don't think they'll let him play until he's five." He threw the lettuce into a colander and ran cold water over it. Just this one last thing, he thought, and they could relax for a few minutes before dinner. The rest of the makings for the Caesar salad were already chopped, blended, and ready, as was the pasta which he'd put in the refrigerator to chill. He'd kept the menu simple so he could concentrate on Sharron. Shutting off the water, he grabbed a couple of clean towels from a bottom drawer and spread the lettuce on them.

"So what's Harry doing in bed already?" she asked. "It's not even dark out yet." She leaned an elbow on the counter, cupping her chin in her palm.

"Six-thirty is his usual bedtime. Harry's always needed at least twelve hours sleep or he doesn't function."

"How do you know he's not playing tiddlywinks under his bed?"

"Trust me, Sharron, he's asleep. Nothing short of a bomb, or the doorbell, will wake him now." He stopped what he was doing to look at her. "You thought Harry was going to eat with us, didn't you?"

She nodded.

"I gave Harry his dinner an hour ago. I'm afraid it's just the two of us." So that was her excuse for wearing a simple cotton dress, not a fancy silk one. Harry.

It amazed Griff that she could be such a wild combination of innocence and daring sensuality. On the one hand, her easy blushes charmed him, as did the way she trembled beneath the simplest touch.

On the other, she'd teased him with the skill of a woman used to teasing.

I'll shave, honey, he'd said. *Your skin is too sensitive, and I might not remember to be careful with you.*

I'll come anyway.

He found himself wanting her with a passion that was startling in its intensity. Wanting her, needing her.

"You can go look in on him if you like. He's not contagious," he reminded her.

She shook her head. "That's all right. I don't want to wake him."

"I don't think that's possible." He threw the lettuce into a wooden bowl, then dried his hands on a towel, his gaze finding hers and holding it. "He still makes a pretty effective chaperon, though. The chance of his waking up and wandering downstairs will keep things from getting too . . . involved."

"That's not what I was thinking."

"Yes, you were." His eyes narrowed on the pulse beating wildly at her throat. "But not even Harry will stop me from kissing you tonight."

A tiny gasp parted her lips.

"Does that make you nervous, Sharron?" he asked.

"A little."

He nodded slowly, examining her with a gaze that was frankly approving. "Excited, too, I think."

She gulped, then surprised him with a whispered "yes" that sizzled the air between them.

"Why?" He liked being the man who excited her.

"I guess I'm not used to being with . . . a man who talks like you do," she finally said, nibbling at her bottom lip.

He hid his grin. Sharron wasn't much used to men, period. That much was becoming more clear with every moment he spent with her. "I remember you saying some pretty outrageous things yourself."

She blushed. "There's a difference, though. I blurt things out pretty much without thinking. You say them deliberately."

He gave an acknowledging nod. "There is a time and place for innuendo. This isn't it." He watched her slender fingers flutter over her skin to settle on the pulse at her throat, then captured her gaze with his own. "We're consenting adults, Sharron. I see no reason to dance around the fact that there's a very strong sexual attraction between us. The only thing left to decide is what we're going to do about it."

Having dropped that bomb, Griff turned to pull the steaks from the refrigerator, then excused himself to put them on the grill. Thankful for the respite, Sharron watched from the stool as he fiddled with the screen door for several moments before it skidded open with a bang in accompaniment to Griff's muffled curse.

She watched his every movement, but her thoughts had nothing to do with what he was doing. She couldn't get her mind off what he'd just said.

The excitement he'd so recently kindled was diminished by a disappointment she couldn't ignore. Diminished, softened . . . but not altogether extinguished. She couldn't take exception to what he'd said—but she'd be lying if she denied the sexual attraction between them. Was it so wrong, she wondered, to hope for something more?

He came back inside, pulling the screen door closed with a rough jerk. His glance slid over her, then returned for a closer inspection. "You're upset. What is it, Sharron?"

She cleared her throat and tried to keep her voice steady. "My lack of experience is showing. I've never had a strictly sexual relationship before. I'm not sure—"

"If sex was all there was to this, you wouldn't be here." He reached for his wineglass and drank from it without taking his gaze from hers. "But we're getting ahead of ourselves, I think. Why don't we have dinner before we talk about if and how we're going to approach our . . . relationship."

"If?"

His expression was mildly reproving. "Nothing's been decided yet, honey. It's not my intention to seduce you off your feet and onto your back without giving both of us a chance to know what we're getting into."

"We're going to talk about it?" she said in a voice that was much higher than she would have liked.

"Um-hmm. That way, neither of us is left guessing." He smiled lazily. "Besides, I don't really intend to seduce you at all. I prefer to think that sex between us will be a joint engagement."

She took several deep, calming breaths that didn't succeed in calming her at all. "Why do I get the feeling I'm more than a little out of my depth with you, Griff?"

"You're not." He leaned back against the counter and folded his arms over his chest. "But I'll make you a deal, honey. I won't tease you about your kissing acquaintance with innocence if you don't let my experience get in the way either."

"How experienced are you, Griff?"

"Enough." Griff's heart slammed against his chest as he struggled with the arousal she'd provoked with her question. *How experienced?* she'd asked, the curious excitement in her voice a trigger that pushed his reactions to her into overload. The little witch didn't have a clue how much effort he was expending to keep from taking her right there on the kitchen counter.

But he'd promised he wouldn't. Not yet. "I'm eight years older than you are, Sharron—"

"How do you know that?" she interrupted.

"Harry. He let it slip the other day." He waved away her miffed protests at Harry's tattling and resumed the subject at hand before it got away from them. "Eight years isn't that much difference, Sharron. But my life has been spent in the real world, not isolated in some music room or on stage." He paused, then added, "If two people are meant to be lovers, experience and innocence are essentially irrelevant."

He kept his expression noncommittal as she hesitated, her face a charming betrayal of her thoughts. Excitement, nervousness, eagerness. They were just the tip of the emotions he saw. She was more shy than he'd expected, yet there was boldness there too.

In Sharron, the combination was wantonly erotic . . . and she didn't even know it.

Her gaze suddenly lifted from his and skipped past his shoulder. "The fire—"

"You think I don't feel it?" he growled, fisting his hands as her words nudged his self-control to the edge. He should have gotten it over with before now, their first kiss. But he'd convinced himself it could wait, until later, when the day's light was gone. In the moonlight, he would take her in his arms, caress her naked shoulders with his lips . . . and discover the warm, honeyed depths of her mouth.

He wasn't sure they'd eat at all if he kissed her now.

He felt his body shudder in sweet anticipation. "Oh

yeah, I feel it, honey. Do you know that I don't remember ever wanting a woman quite like this before? I look at you and I think I'll go mad with that wanting. I hear your voice and I get so hard that I can hardly think straight." He leveled a hot, hungry stare on her. "If I'm so experienced, Sharron, then why am I having to work so hard to control this fire that burns for you inside of me?"

Sharron stared at him, her heart doing double time as bolts of pleasure shot through her. Fire, he'd said, and meant it. She knew, because she was feeling the same thing. *Fire*, she remembered suddenly, moaning with frustration as she pointed toward the patio. "The *fire*, Griff. The *barbecue!*"

He quirked a puzzled eyebrow, then looked over his shoulder. "Dammit! Why didn't you tell me before?" he muttered, striding quickly toward the door.

The screen door jammed, refusing this time to slide open at all. Uttering something short and obscene, Griff took a step back, lifted his foot, and slammed it against the metal frame. Overwhelmed by the show of force, the door shuddered, then surrendered in a back flip onto the patio. Griff ignored the residual clattering of metal on stone as he strode across the flagstones and tackled the flames.

Blithely disregarding his inference that the fire was in any way her fault, Sharron watched Griff, spellbound by his sudden, controlled violence . . . fascinated by the ensuing calm.

Without fuss, he covered the grill with the domed lid. After waiting a few seconds for the flames to extinguish, he opened it again and poked at the steaks with a long fork. Evidently satisfied no lasting harm had been done, he turned and headed back to the house, pausing to pick up the screen door and prop it against the wall.

There was a look of chagrin on his face as he resumed his position across the counter. "I've been meaning to do something about that door since we moved in."

She had trouble hiding her grin. "Don't you think it was a little overmatched?"

"It was the steaks or the door," he said, grinning too. "The door lost."

"How did the steaks fare?"

"They're nearly done. Singed, but otherwise coming along fine." He shot her a reproving glance. "You could have told me about the fire sooner."

"I did. You chose not to listen."

His eyebrows lifted in conspicuous disappointment. "So that was what you were talking about," he said, moving around the counter until he was standing beside her. His hands went to her waist, and he pulled her off the stool and against his body. It was a long slide downward, a journey that left her intimately aware of every hard, muscled part of him. When, finally, her toes touched the floor, he settled an arm around her waist to keep her close and cupped her chin with his hand, his long fingers spreading across her jaw.

"I was going to wait until after dinner for this," he said, bending down until his lips were just a breath from hers. "But I don't think I can sit across the table from you and wonder anymore."

"If you'll like kissing me?" she asked, her lips brushing

against his, her hands slipping past his shoulders to lock behind his neck.

He gave a low, ferocious growl. "No, honey. I know I'll like it. I just want to know how much."

His mouth lowered to hers, taking the gasp that parted her lips as an invitation to come inside. He opened her mouth wide beneath his, his tongue stroking the length of hers in a lazy exploration that elicited tiny moans of surprise, then unaffected pleasure from the woman in his arms. She was honey and wine, and he found himself drowning in her, the rough beat of his heart following him headlong into the whirlpool of her exotic taste.

She knew how to kiss because he was teaching her as he went. Her shy, tentative responses sharpened with each new thrust of his tongue. She became more adept at anticipating, following his lead with an enthusiasm that nearly swept him over the edge.

A place they weren't yet ready to go.

He retreated from her mouth to brush soft, tender kisses on her lips, his thumb tracing her swollen lower lip. "Now I know what you really look like when you've just been kissed," he murmured, dropping a kiss on her nose before pulling her arms from around his neck. He backed away slowly, conscious of her gaze on the hardness that pressed against his zipper. "You felt it, didn't you? Pressing against you, just like I could feel your hard nipples against my chest."

Her gaze flew to his face, and she made a strangled sound that he interpreted as part embarrassment, part laughter at getting caught staring. He had to give her credit, though, that she didn't raise her hands to cover her breasts. He rubbed the back of his neck in an attempt to dispel some of the tension that had settled there and managed to get the counter between them before she went cross-eyed from avoiding looking at his crotch.

She climbed back onto the stool and fixed him with a smile so outrageous, he nearly chucked all plans for dinner. "I think you do that on purpose."

"What's that?"

"Embarrass me." The pink tip of her tongue came out to moisten her lips. He watched, captivated, remembering a moment ago when it had been writhing beneath his. "It gives you the upper hand."

He laughed and shook his head. "Sorry to disappoint you. I say what I mean, nothing less."

"Then perhaps the next time I tell you there's a fire, you'll believe what I say instead of jumping to conclusions."

He dropped his gaze to her breasts where the nipples were still poking against the cotton dress. "Oh, I don't really think I jumped to any conclusions. Do you?"

She picked an apple from the fruit bowl and threw it at him. Griff caught it easily, his laughter a tonic for the discomfort he was still enduring in the area of his groin. "Speaking of fires, honey, we need to finish up here and eat before those steaks turn into cinder blocks."

Sharron didn't know if she was relieved or disappointed when he began pulling food out of the refrigerator. Just moments ago, the atmosphere in the kitchen had been hot . . . sizzling hot. His kiss had been unlike anything she'd ever experienced. But then, she didn't have a vast inventory to compare it to.

Somehow, though, she knew Griff's kiss wouldn't suffer upon comparison.

"Another glass of wine with dinner?" he asked, cutting into her thoughts. With a slight flush coloring her cheeks, she nodded.

Griff deliberately didn't touch her as he filled her glass and handed it back to her. There was so much to learn, to understand about this woman whose kisses left him both weak and hard at the same time. Shy one moment, bold the next . . . and claiming to be neither just to confuse him.

Sharron was driving him crazy without even trying.

"How can I help?" she asked.

He grinned and shook his head. "By staying out of the way, I should imagine." It would be for the best, he thought, if she stayed on one side of the counter and he on the other. The arousal she'd incited just minutes ago was barely under control.

An accidental touch, and they might not have dinner after all. Griff made another trip to the refrigerator, then began assembling the salad.

"Are you implying I can't cook?" Hooking the heels of her sandals on the rung of her stool, she folded her arms on the counter and watched him work.

He shot her a teasing glance. "Anyone who can live with a kitchen as small as yours either can't or won't cook. I suspect it's both."

She gave in gracefully. "I have other talents," she said, thinking of her musical skill.

"I'm counting on that."

So much for eschewing innuendo.

They had dinner on the patio beneath the soft light of a hurricane lamp Griff had hung from a low rafter. The evening was quiet and gentle, and the air was filled with the scent of jasmine. Sharron ate with the appreciation of one who loved home cooking and never got any.

Griff kept the conversation light, entertaining her with stories about his parents who were currently fishing the inland waters of Alaska. Hiking, too, he added, although he'd heard rumblings that his mother was getting fed up with the primitive, ice-cold bathing facilities. They lived in northern Wisconsin, he told her, where they ran a small bed and breakfast for the hunting and fishing crowd.

"Is that where you learned to cook?" she asked, twirling the pasta around her fork. "What do you call this anyway? It's terrific."

"Cold pasta in olive oil and fresh basil."

"That's it?"

"I'm not much on fancy names. And no, I didn't learn to cook at the B and B. The folks have only had it a few years." He pushed his empty plate aside and picked up his wineglass, holding the fragile stem in his fingertips. "I taught myself how to cook when I discovered my wife—

ex-wife—wasn't interested. We were in college at the time, and couldn't afford to eat out."

He'd been married. Sharron hadn't realized that. She took another bite of the pasta to keep from asking details that were none of her business.

Griff put his wineglass aside and folded his arms on the table, his gaze meeting hers with an intensity she could almost feel. "I loved my wife, Sharron. Past tense, but while we were married, I was convinced our marriage was one of those happily-ever-after stories."

"You don't have to tell me this," she said softly.

"Yes, I do. It's important you understand." He picked up the steak knife from his plate and focused his attention on its razor-sharp blade. "Janet and I were about to celebrate our fifth anniversary when, quite by accident, I discovered she'd had an abortion the year before."

"Your baby . . . ?" He nodded, a moan of distress escaped her lips. She simply couldn't imagine the pain he must have felt, must still feel. "How could she?"

Griff just shrugged. "That's not the point of this conversation, Sharron. I loved her. I trusted her to share the important decisions with me. I was wrong. When I found out about the abortion, I realized love was a damned silly basis for a marriage."

"Just because one woman—"

"You're not listening." He dropped the knife on the table and captured her hand, spreading her fingers with the tips of his. "A man doesn't have any control over who he falls in love with. History is filled with idiots who loved the wrong woman."

"And vice versa," she murmured.

He acknowledged that with a brief nod. "I decided after the divorce that I'd never trust myself to marry again. My judgment was impaired once. There's nothing to say it wouldn't happen again." His fingers slid between hers, stretching her hand as their palms met. "I won't marry again, Sharron. Not ever. It wouldn't be fair to get involved with you without making that clear."

She curled her fingers into his hand. "It's clear." And rather irrelevant, she mused, given her own decisions. It was the child she was remembering, though, the one that had never breathed.

The pain of that loss filled her with a grief that was strangely personal.

Griff looked up at her from beneath half-closed lids. "It's a tragedy that's long past, Sharron. I only told you because we're getting involved and you deserve to know the truth."

"Do you do this often?"

"Tell people about my marriage?" He shook his head. "No. I meant, do you get involved often?"

His laugh was harsh. "It's been a long time since I've been interested enough in a particular woman to want to spend more than a few evenings in her company."

"How do you know I'll last any longer than that?"

"I know." He turned her hand over until her palm was open to his curious touch. He traced the lines of her life, hesitating over the slight calluses on her fingertips. "You know it too. Every time I touch you, your body responds in ways you have no control over. Right now, for example, we're just holding hands, yet your breasts are swelling in anticipation of a more intimate touch . . . even though I've never touched you there before."

Her gasp drew his gaze to her mouth. "And now, Sharron, you're wondering how much longer it's going to be before we kiss again."

"How did you know?" The whisper parted her lips before she could stop it.

"There are times when your every thought is written on your face in capital letters." He let her hand slip from his, yet held her captive with a deliberately heated gaze. "This is one of those times."

"So that's how you do it. I suppose it's a relief to know you're not a mind reader." She flushed brightly, then touched the linen napkin to her lips. "You'd think a twenty-nine-year-old woman would be sophisticated enough to keep her thoughts to herself."

"There are a few things you've managed to keep private."

"Such as?"

"Why you don't want children." He shifted his chair sideways to the table and stretched out his long legs, crossing them at the ankle. "I've seen you with Harry. You're good with him, yet you act like you don't know what you're doing."

"That's because I don't." She wedged her shoulders into the back cushion of her chair and watched Griff across the rim of her wineglass. She held it cupped in her palms, using both hands because she was still quivering in reaction to the sensual byplay and didn't think she could hold the glass with just one. "I've never been around kids. I think I mentioned that before when we were talking about disgusting diseases."

"Never?"

She shook her head. "The conservatory where I studied when I was younger was filled with serious students, serious parents, and serious teachers who were seriously appalled by frivolous activities. That meant children were to act as adults if they wanted to be there at all. The academy where I finished my studies was much of the same. And from there, I went straight to the concert circuit." She pushed the fingers of one hand through her hair, her nerves easing as the subject of her reactions to his touch was left in the distance. "I know less about children than I do about physics—and I flunked that subject years ago."

"That's all?" he asked, a puzzled expression furrowing his brow. "You aren't accustomed to them, ergo you don't want any?"

She gave a self-conscious laugh. "That, and I have to admit to being protective of my independence. I'm pretty set in my ways now, and I can't imagine altering my life to the extent that children would have a comfortable place in it." She lowered her voice to a reminiscent hum. "My mom was forever telling me how much her life changed when I was born. Before then, she'd assumed a child was nothing more than another body to work into the schedule. It was a rude surprise when she discovered babies and children don't acknowledge schedules."

"It's my understanding that teenagers are even worse,"

he murmured, grinning wryly. "I can't tell you how much I'm looking forward to those years."

"Don't give me any of that nonsense, Griffen Ross. You love children. Anyone who sees you with Harry can tell parenting is something you're very good at. You'll handle his teenage tantrums and love it."

He acknowledged her comment with a snort of disbelief that carried with it an unmistakable hint of contentment. "So if you're serious about not having children, is marriage also out of the question?"

"Not at all. I'm sure there are a few good men left who are as set in their ways as I am." She lifted her left hand and wiggled her long fingers in the low light of the lamp. "I'm not in a hurry, though. Putting a ring on this finger will have to be more than a matter of convenience." And that, she decided, was enough on the subject of children and marriage.

"Tell me, Griff," she went on, cocking her head as she stared at him with unstoppable curiosity, "do you grill all your dates like this?"

"Not to worry, honey. The steaks got singed because I wasn't paying attention. That's why all the questions. I want to make sure neither of us gets . . . burned."

An involuntary laugh burst from her at the dreadful pun, but it wasn't laughter that she saw in Griff's gaze, which was suddenly dark and serious.

It was something else altogether. Her breath caught in her throat as her laughter died in the night's soft air.

"So what do you think, Sharron?" he asked, his voice a low murmur that she had to strain to hear. "Can we be lovers . . . and friends . . . without making the mistake of wanting more?"

"I think I'd like to try," she said, hiding her hands under the table so he couldn't see their trembling.

"You just think?" His brows waggled in mock amusement.

A fiendish spirit made her lay down a challenge. "You've only kissed me once, Griff. True, it was fairly spectacular . . . but how do I know it wasn't a fluke?"

SEVEN

It wasn't a fluke. Nor was their second kiss anything like their first.

Griff's mouth was on Sharron's almost before she realized he'd moved. One moment he was sitting across from her, his expression enigmatic as her challenge lay sweet and precarious between them. In the next breath, he was beside her, bending down to capture her mouth beneath his. His tongue thrust inside, retreated, then thrust again, his lips hard against hers in a kiss that was assertive and assured.

When he was done taking the kiss—yes, taking, because he hadn't allowed her a chance to give—he captured her chin in his fingers so that she had no choice but to meet his stare. "It wasn't a fluke, honey. And spectacular doesn't even begin to describe it."

Without blinking, she lifted a hand to her mouth, her fingers skating lightly across her swollen lips. Then she touched those same fingers to his mouth, smiling tentatively when he flinched but didn't move away. It reassured her to know that he was as sensitive to her touch as she was to his. "I can see I'll have to be more careful with what I say."

He drew the tip of one of her fingers into his mouth, biting lightly before letting go. "As much as I'd enjoy taming that mouth of yours, I have to admit I'd rather not. The suspense of wondering what you'll say next puts an edge on things that's remarkably provocative."

He hesitated, then asked point-blank what he needed to know. "So what is it, Sharron. Are we going to be lovers or not?"

She smiled. "And friends, Griff. I need that too."

"So do I, honey." He leaned down and brushed his lips across hers once more before turning to stack their dishes. His hands were full as he headed toward the kitchen. "I need to check on Harry. Be right back."

Sharron waited until she was sure he was on his way upstairs before moving. Standing on legs that were certifiably shaky, she gathered what was left on the table, concentrating on the task at hand in a deliberate attempt to block out any and all thoughts relating to the man upstairs.

It wouldn't do her any good to think, not now . . . when it was too late for second thoughts. All that was left was to enjoy, and hope to heaven that her heart came out of this arrangement between them reasonably intact.

She was rinsing the remnants of dinner from their plates when Griff descended from his son's room. "I wish I slept that deeply," he said as he rounded the counter and began to put the things she'd rinsed into the dishwasher. "Some nights when I go into his room, I put my ear to his heart just to make sure he's even breathing."

She stopped what she was doing as his words touched something deep inside. "It must be terrifying, having someone who depends on you for absolutely everything. I think I'd never sleep for worrying."

Griff shot her a surprised glance. "You get used to it," he said, then looked away in confusion. For a woman who claimed to know nothing about children, she was remarkably intuitive about the harsh realities.

He wondered if she was even remotely aware of the flip side of the coin—the joy and laughter that only children could inspire.

She laughed self-consciously and dried her hands on a towel, then used it to wipe down the sink. "If he sleeps so well at night, why does he still nap in the afternoon?"

Griff took the towel from her and threw it on the counter, then caught her hand and pulled her toward the darkened living room. "I'm afraid that naps are very nearly a thing of the past. Lately I've begun to realize he's only taking them to humor me." He led her to a sofa that was just out of sight of the stairs leading to the second level and tugged her down beside him without bothering to turn on the lights. His arm slid around her shoulders and pulled her gently against his side.

Her awareness of him heightened, but in a totally nonsexual way. It was comfortable being this close; comforting. She snuggled closer, resting her cheek on his chest as his hand caressed her arm in long, even strokes.

He was going to make love to her, she knew. Not tonight, not with Harry just upstairs. It would be soon, though. Griff didn't seem like a man who would deny himself for any longer than absolutely necessary.

It was like their first kiss—the anticipation was driving her crazy.

She closed her eyes, the steady heartbeat beneath her ear lulling her into a state of semiconscious awareness. She'd never been this close to a man before and felt so totally at ease, she thought, taking a deep breath that sounded even to her ears like a yawn.

Griff didn't appear to notice, or didn't care if he did, because he just tightened his arm around her shoulders and continued the steady stroking of his hand. Slipping out of her shoes, Sharron tucked her legs beneath her and allowed her mind to drift over the events of the evening.

He teased her unconscionably, yet there was a method to his teasing. He wanted her, and wanted her to know it.

He'd kissed her, giving her a taste of how exquisite their lovemaking would be.

He'd warned her against forever, presenting her with the reasons forever could never happen. She believed him. On her side, Harry was a powerful motivator that would keep her from wanting more than Griff was offering.

"Sharron?"

"Hmm?"

"Are you on the pill?

Her eyes flew open, and she would have rocketed out of his arms had he not exerted the pressure to keep her where she was. The low rumble of his laugh muddied the beat of his heart, and she could only be glad he couldn't see the blush that covered her face.

She was tired of blushing every other time he opened his mouth.

"Well?" he prodded, giving her a little shake. "Are you or aren't you."

"I'm not."

"Damn!" he said softly, the imprecation having all the more force for its lack of volume. "Can you take it? I mean, is there any physical reason you can't?"

She shook her head against his chest. "I can. I have. I've just not had any reason to, not lately . . ." Birth control hadn't been on the agenda in so long, she'd not given any thought to it. "Can't you, er, do something about it?"

"I can, honey. And I will, if that's what you'd prefer." He shifted her, his hands coaxing her feet out from under her. He lifted her legs to rest across his thighs and forced her chin up until her head was cradled in the crook of his arm. They stared at each other in the muted light that filtered in from the kitchen.

"I know that making love with you is going to be . . . intense," he said, smiling over the word. "I'd hate to take the chance of your getting pregnant just because I forgot to protect you in the heat of the moment."

"I see what you mean," she whispered, feeling a little like the screen door—overwhelmed. "I'll see a doctor about it."

"Good." His kiss was hard and approving.

Sharron tugged at her skirt, which had ridden far too high above her knees. He captured her hands and held them flat against his chest. "If you want to fidget, do it here, where I can feel it."

"You want me to touch you?" she whispered.

"Mm-hmm." He guided her fingers to the buttons of his shirt, leaving it for her to decide whether to open them or just slide her fingers between the gaps. His hand stroked the back of hers, silently encouraging as she thought about how much she wanted just that—to feel his hands on her. It filled her with wonder that he would want the same. She tried to get a little closer, so that her reach was more comfortable, scooting a few inches across his thighs, her fanny rubbing against his hip until his arm tightened around her shoulders and forced her to be still.

"Settle down, honey. All that wiggling is having an effect on me that's as untimely as it is uncomfortable." Leaving her fingers hooked between the buttons of his shirt, he stroked the smooth line of her shoulder, his fingers tripping lightly over the strap of her dress. "I'm so hard now, it's all I can do not to flip your skirt over your hips and find out how deep inside you I can go."

Her fingers curled around a button and popped it loose before she realized what was happening. Damn his teasing mouth, she thought, and wished he'd do something more constructive than tease.

She wanted him to kiss her again.

He was too busy watching her, she realized. Watching her hands on his chest . . . following the path of his own hand as it inched aside the strap of her dress. With trembling fingers, she smoothed his shirt back down as if the button were still fastened, then went to work on the next.

What was the harm in touching? she thought, a delicate shiver overcoming her as she felt Griff's fingers nudge the strap across her shoulder and down her arm. As long as they remembered that was all they could do.

"It's just as well we have a chaperon, isn't it?" she asked, her voice not quite steady as he ran a finger along the gathered seam of her dress. She took a deep breath, unfastening a second button and smoothing the cloth before moving down to the next. "If I remember correctly, once I start taking the pills, it'll be a while before they kick in." Not to mention how long it would take to get an appointment with the doctor, she mused, then decided that come hell or high water, she'd get it done the next day.

"Between now and then, will you trust me to protect you?" He touched the side of her face. "Or would you prefer to wait?"

She swallowed over the hard lump in her throat. "Harry's just upstairs. If he found us . . ."

"I didn't mean tonight, honey." His warm breath caressed her forehead. "I wouldn't dream of making love with you with Harry just upstairs. The things we're going to do together require more privacy than we've got now."

Her nerves quivered as her imagination soared, and she buried her face against his chest.

He let her hide there for scarcely a moment before digging his fingers into her hair and drawing back her head. "I didn't say you had to stop touching me, Sharron."

She took a deep breath, rubbing her hands against his shirt as an unfamiliar boldness filled her with daring. "Think you can handle it?"

"I'll handle it," he said, his voice a hoarse rumble as his little finger stroked the sensitive nerves at the top of her spine.

She shivered and tackled his shirt with less hesitation than before. When four buttons were undone, she took the occasion to open his shirt. Her fingertips raked through the light dusting of dark blond hair that curled there, skimmed around the tight buds of his nipples . . . then homed in when he groaned and she knew it was what he wanted.

His hips bucked under her thighs, leaving her in no doubt that if they'd had the required privacy, he would be naked and thrusting inside her before she could catch her next breath. He kissed her, a long, devouring kiss that made her fingers curl against his chest. His heat surrounded her, and the frustration of wanting without having brought a moan to her lips. She gave another cry when his mouth caressed the sensitive skin of her neck.

Griff knew then that he wasn't sending her home, not yet. His fingers went to her mouth, hushing her cries as his lips continued to explore her soft satin skin.

She buried her face in his chest, her heated breath flaying him with reminders of what couldn't happen. Griff tightened his arm around her shoulders and pulled her away.

There was only so much temptation he could stand.

"Honey?" He tucked his knuckles under her chin, forcing her to look at him.

"What?"

"Let me make love to you."

"We can't." Her smile was filled with regret.

"I can." He kissed her parted lips, then tangled his hand in her hair and slowly pulled her head back to expose the long line of her neck. "I can, and I think I have to."

"But what about . . ." Her words faded as his mouth found the pulse that beat a frantic rhythm at the base of her throat.

"A one-way street, honey," he said, his fingers looping around the other strap of her dress and tugging it aside. "There's nothing to worry about."

He knew she understood when she stiffened, then suddenly began to struggle in his arms. He controlled her struggles with one hand on the bare skin of her thighs and an arm locked just beneath her breasts, his mouth heavy on hers. Her struggles ceased after a short moment. She looked at him with such mingled emotions in her expression that it was all he could do not to pull her close and calm her with words of comfort.

"I can't, Griff," she said, her voice a mere whisper between them, her eyes filled with fear of the unknown. "I've never—"

"Never taken without giving?" he interrupted, wanting only to get past the words so they could begin. He'd expected her to be shy about allowing him to pleasure her without taking anything in return. But he wasn't going to let it stop him from giving her this small gift.

"It seems so . . . selfish," she murmured. "And Harry—"

"Harry won't intrude." His hand at her thighs relaxed from its restraining grip, the fingers spreading across skin that was like quivering velvet beneath his touch. "And I'll still be dressed. If he does awaken, I'll know it before he can get down the stairs."

She opened her mouth to protest again, and he covered it with his own. She'd agreed to be his lover, he told himself. He needed to do this now, to give her something to remember in case second thoughts overwhelmed her after she left him that night.

She gave into his needs, into her own, with a gentle sigh. He felt her body relax, and before their kiss was done, he was assured he hadn't seduced her into something she didn't want.

He'd seduced her into wanting something she'd never known.

He took care to learn her taste, her responses—her mouth, how she kissed, the soft cries that he swallowed before they traveled too far. Her breasts, round and full, swelled against him, their hard tips stroking his chest from behind the barrier of cotton. When she tried to push the shirt from his shoulders, he took her hands and forced them around his neck where they could do the least harm.

A one-way street, he'd told her. He meant to keep his word.

He edged her against the corner of the sofa so he

didn't have to support her shoulders with his arm, leaving both hands free to discover the tender secrets of her body. He kept one hand at her thighs, which were still draped across his lap, stroking her casually, getting her used to his touch so that she wouldn't be surprised when he introduced a greater intimacy.

His lips followed the path of his other hand as it explored the soft contours of her shoulders, the gentle rise of her breasts . . . the sensitive tips that were still hidden behind her bright summer dress. He took his time, toying with the tender hollows on the inside of her elbow, delighting in her moans as his tongue traced the delicate swirl of her ear.

She responded without restraint, giving him more pleasure than she could ever have imagined.

Griff took another kiss, then hooked his fingers in her dress . . . in the valley between her breasts . . . and tugged.

His hand flexed around her thigh as her rose-tipped breasts were slowly exposed. She gave a little cry, so scft that he didn't worry about it waking Harry. But when he put his lips on one rosy nipple and took it into his mouth, she cried out again. He massaged her lips with his fingers, muffling her cries as he began to lick at the sensitive nub. She squirmed in his lap, not fighting him but wanting more and not knowing how to get it.

Griff knew. Releasing the one breast from his attention, he turned to the other and began to push her thighs open with the steady pressure of his hand. The shyness in her argued with him, though, silently denying him by keeping her legs squeezed together. He laughed at her impudence and sucked hard at her breast.

Her legs fell apart, and his hand slid upward, finding the barrier of her panties. He stroked her through the nylon, knowing better than Sharron what would excite her and what wouldn't. She squirmed and shifted, and when she finally found his mouth with her own, he realized she needed the anchor of their joined mouths. She was so close to the edge.

His tongue found hers just as his fingers slipped beneath her panties to caress the swollen flower of her passion. Her cries filled his mouth, and his fingers became coated in the slick evidence of her excitement. He leaned into her, stroking her breasts with his chest, her tongue with his tongue, her slippery heat with a poor substitute for the rock-hard arousal between his thighs. He stroked her and entered her tight sheath with one finger, then two. His thumb found the tender nub that was nearly hidden beneath her soft, springy curls, and he blanked his mind as he began a slow torment of her most sensitive place.

She fell apart in stages. Finally, he thought, but knew it had only been scant minutes since they'd begun. Her response was phenomenal in its intensity, complete and unreserved.

Another moment, though, and he would have had to join her. Inside her heat, the length of him savoring the pulse of her climax.

Not tonight.

It was good, though, even from a semiparticipant's

point of view. He watched her face grow taut as her body was slowly overtaken by a quivering she couldn't control. She clenched around his fingers, then did it again as he deliberately strummed her swollen nub with his thumb. He grinned, then lowered his mouth to her breast because the tip was so hard, he couldn't help but wonder if she'd like his teeth around it. She did.

When her tremors had ceased, he used his hands and mouth to calm her, stroking her thighs without teasing, kissing her breasts in praise instead of passion.

She wound her arms more tightly around his neck and filled his ears with such nonsense, it was all he could do not to laugh.

He didn't, though, because she was only telling him how much she'd liked it . . . and why couldn't she do the same to him, more or less?

She couldn't, he told her, because he knew himself better than to imagine he could allow her hands on his body without wanting to bury himself where his fingers had so recently explored.

At least, he told her, not the first time.

She lay against the corner of the sofa and let him put her clothes back in place without arguing further, although he worried about the glint of revenge he saw in her eyes.

It was an exciting kind of worry that he knew would keep him awake deep into the long hours of the night. He slipped her feet into the discarded sandals, then sat back to admire the picture she made—mussed and satisfied and a little sleepy.

He was tempted to begin it all over again.

"You don't play fair," she told him, sitting up and dragging her fingers through her hair in an attempt to make sense of the tangles he'd put there.

"I wasn't playing, Sharron," he managed to reply, his voice a gruff bark that should have warned her he was too close to the edge to tease. "What you gave me tonight will fill my dreams for the next week." He caught her wrists in his hands and drew them to her sides. Turning her around, he proceeded to finish the job of straightening her hair for her, filling his hands with the silk and imagining what it would feel like spread across his thighs. . . . His heart slammed against his chest as he put that fantasy aside for another time.

"And what about my dreams, Griff?" she asked as he walked her to the door.

He'd have to teach her not to tease . . . someday. For now, though, he swung her around and backed her against the front door, sliding between her thighs so that she could feel the hardness between his. "Walk back to the couch with me, honey, and I'll make you so tired you won't have the energy to dream."

Her chest filled with air that didn't help her to breathe at all. "I can't," she said, staring at him. "I want all of you," she whispered.

He kissed her gently, mindful of her swollen lips. "I know, honey. But do me a favor, hmm?"

"What?"

"See the doctor tomorrow. I was serious about what I said before. I don't want to take chances about leaving protection to strength of mind." He grabbed a set of keys from the ledge by the door and thrust them into her hand. "Take the car," he added, gesturing to the vehicle that was parked in the driveway. "It's too late for you to walk, and I can't leave Harry."

She took the keys without argument and headed down the stairs. Griff watched from the door, catching his breath as she stepped through a moonbeam that filled her hair with a shimmering white light. Then she was in the shadows again, opening the door to his car.

"I'll call in five minutes," he called across the lawn in a low voice.

She turned. "Don't trust me with your car, Griff?"

"Humor me, honey, and go straight home." He leaned against the doorjamb, folding his arms across his chest. "I'd hate to waste the night worrying about you when I could be fantasizing about how good it's going to be when I come inside you."

"Keep your voice down, Griffen Ross," she said, glancing over her shoulder at the empty street. "Do you want your neighbors to hear?"

"Make that fifteen minutes, honey. Five to get home and ten to take your clothes off and get into bed." His low laugh mated with her gasp.

"If you don't care about your neighbors, then at least think of Harry—"

"All your clothes, Sharron. And turn off the lights so you can pretend I'm there with you." In the moonlight, her expression was so priceless, it was all he could do not to close the distance between them and kiss away the outrage. "Now be a good girl and leave before I—"

She slid into the car and slammed the door before he could finish.

Just as well, he mused, watching as she backed out of the driveway. He really didn't have any idea how he'd complete that threat.

Touching her again would have been the end of control.

"Regrets, honey?"

Sharron changed the phone to her other ear and rolled onto her side so she could see the willow just beyond her terrace. She'd planted it herself, eight years ago when she'd bought the house. Now it was as tall as her home, its branches graceful and strong in the night's gentle breeze. There was something mysterious about the willow in moonlight, an enchantment of sorts that disappeared with the light of day.

Just as she was afraid that the sense of intimacy, of rightness, between her and Griff would transform come daylight into something quite ordinary.

"Sharron?"

"I'm here." Yes, she thought, she was there. All one hundred and ten shy, miserable pounds of her. She'd burned, then melted under his touch, revealing a wanton side of herself she'd never encountered. *How had he known it was there?*

"I asked if you had any regrets."

"No." No regrets. She'd wallowed in his caresses, followed his touch across the heavens until the stars had burst in a three-dimensional explosion of Technicolor delight. *She'd wanted to see the stars with him.*

His deep laugh filled her senses. "I do, honey. Want to hear about it?"

"You have regrets?" Her heart slammed against her chest.

"Only that I had to send you home. Do you have any idea how hard that was for me?"

A sigh escaped her lips. "I feel so strange, Griff—"

"I know you do. You were so high one minute, giving everything of yourself, coming apart in my hands . . . the next I was rushing you out the door." His voice deepened with the memory. "I should have kept you here, held you until you'd touched earth again. But I couldn't, not without wanting to let you fly again. Not without needing to go with you."

She smiled in the moonlight, and something tickled her heart into that rhythm that she was beginning to recognize as Griff-pattern madness. "So that's what's wrong. And here I was thinking I'd eaten something that disagreed with me."

His laughter was rich and full. "I'll teach you to belittle my cooking, wench. Come over tomorrow night and I'll let you have your way with my kitchen."

Tomorrow night. She hadn't expected to see him again so soon. It was so fast, this thing that was happening between them. She didn't know if she could keep up with the pace he set . . . or if it was wise to try.

She found herself agreeing without waiting for the answers to her own private questions. "I'll come and show you how to order pizza."

"Come, and I'll teach you how to make it," he countered.

She smiled in the darkness, thinking Griff really didn't know what he was getting into. "Okay." They agreed to make it an early dinner—Harry's favorite food was pizza—then she rolled onto her other side so that she could hang up the phone when he said good night.

Twenty minutes later, he still hadn't said it . . . and Sharron realized she couldn't do it either.

It was as close to spending the night together as they could get.

EIGHT

If she'd known how difficult it was going to be, she wouldn't have tried it.

It also would have made more sense if she'd worn shorts. Or trousers. Anything but the summer skirt that she had to tame with one hand so she could see the really important stuff.

Like her feet.

Maybe they were too big, she considered, eyeing the size sixes that shuffled precariously along the wall an inch at a time. Harry hadn't had this much trouble, she remembered, and his feet were much smaller.

Nor was Sharron forgetting the fact she had farther to fall than did a three-and-a-half-year-old child. Glaring malevolently at a rosebush that looked as though it was planning to jump out and grab her as she passed, she wadded her skirt more firmly into one hand and edged by it, then negotiated another ten feet of wall.

The front walk would have been so much simpler. But

then she'd have to ring the front bell—if she could find it—and that was precisely what she was trying to avoid.

Asking to borrow Harry would expose a side of her to Griff that she had no intention of exposing. On top of which, she thought it best to avoid Griff. Daylight had succeeded in whittling away at her confidence, and she was just the slightest bit unnerved by what had transpired between them.

Had she really lain in his arms, half naked and mindless under his skilled hands? Sharron blushed, then shoved aside the vivid image.

She had other fish to fry.

The point of this exercise was to snatch Harry from his own backyard and put him back before Griff noticed. She knew he was out there playing. Griff had given her that information not ten minutes ago, calling from the kitchen, where he kept an eye on his son who was digging holes in the flower bed. Yes, he'd assured her, Harry was well enough to be outside. The fresh air was good for him, and he needed the exercise.

He'd called to find out if she'd been to the doctor. She had, and his husky praise had sent her pulse soaring. Then he'd told her to bring her own anchovies for the pizza because it wasn't a topping either he or Harry liked. She'd been on the point of asking where she could buy some—never having shopped for anchovies before—when the call-waiting on his telephone had beeped and he'd rung off. She'd decided to do without.

Sharron stared down the length of the rock wall and

wondered what Griff would say when she called from the hospital with a broken whatever.

Even worse, he might discover Harry was gone before she put him back. If that should happen, Plan A was to feign innocence . . . and blame it all on Harry. Say he'd come over on his own accord.

Harry never got into trouble.

That solution in hand, she fretted that Harry might have gone inside. That would mean she'd have to return home empty-handed. On the wall, she realized with a grimace, conceding a critical flaw in her plan.

"Hi, Shawon!"

Bingo! One child in the garden. Not daring to look up from her feet, she crept another few inches until her peripheral vision encountered a place where green lawn verged on the wall. She leapt down and was congratulating herself on the two-point landing when she looked up to find Harry sitting in his father's lap.

So much for a subtle snatch.

"Er, hello, Harry," she mumbled, focusing on the bundle of speed and light that jumped down from Griff's lap and plowed into her knees. Without sparing a look from whence he came—she just couldn't look at Griff, not yet—Sharron unlocked the chubby arms and knelt down to renew their acquaintance. Dressed in a typical outfit, this time lime-green shirt over pink shorts, he looked pretty good for a kid who'd been sick for a week. She examined his arms and legs, finding sores that were well along in the healing process.

"You're looking pretty good, kiddo," she said, noting

with relief the disease had bypassed his face. "I thought you were supposed to be sick."

He giggled and wrapped his arms around her neck. "I *was* sick, Shawon. With the pox."

"Chicken pox," she corrected him.

"That's what I said. The pox." He leaned close to confide, "Be glad you didn't get it, Shawon. It itches in places you wouldn't like."

She choked back a giggle. "I'm sure it does."

They cuddled for a couple of minutes, Sharron forgetting their audience as she wallowed in Harry's tight hug. When he relaxed his hold and leaned back, she gave him a quick kiss on his cheek. "I'm glad you're okay, Harry."

"Want to play on the swings with me?" he asked, accepting her arrival with the aplomb of one who used the wall as an ordinary means of transportation.

A deeper voice interrupted. "Not now, Harry. I want to talk to Sharron for a bit. Why don't you go ahead, and I'll come push you in a minute."

"Okay." Harry scurried across the yard to the swing set as Sharron slowly got up off her knees. When she could no longer avoid it, she lifted her gaze to find Griff staring at her, a puzzled expression furrowing his brow.

"What are you afraid of, honey?" he asked quietly, waving a hand to the adjoining chair in an invitation to sit. "Why are you having so much trouble looking at me?"

She sighed and sank into the lawn chair, then buried her face in her hands. "I want so much to be sophisticated about this!" she wailed.

She didn't hear him move to kneel in front of her

chair, but she knew he was there. Gentle hands pulled her fingers from her eyes. With his knuckles beneath her chin, Griff forced her to face him. Sharron looked into dark brown eyes that were filled with tender understanding and wanted to cry.

"What do you want to be sophisticated about?" he asked.

"About us."

"How?" His hand slipped around her neck, his fingers spreading upward into her hair.

"I can't look at you without remembering last night," she whispered. "I can't even think about you without . . . thinking about it."

His eyebrows raised in mild curiosity. "You think it would be more sophisticated to pretend it didn't happen?"

She nodded briskly. "It would be better, wouldn't it? I mean, how can I function if every time I look at you . . . I see stars?"

Griff stared at her for a long time before answering. "Do you have any idea how much pleasure you gave me last night?"

"I didn't do anythi—"

His fingers covered her lips, and he shook his head in gentle rebuke. "You gave me pleasure. By watching you, being with you, I saw those same stars." His fingers traced the line of her lips as his other hand pushed her head forward to meet his. "If it's not sophisticated to be filled with that memory, then perhaps being sophisticated isn't something either of us needs to worry about." His mouth touched hers in a kiss that was tender and warm.

"You too?" she murmured as he sat back on his heels.

He nodded gravely. "Me too."

She let out a huge sigh of relief and smiled. "I'm glad we got that out of the way. I was kind of nervous about facing you at dinner."

He slid back into his chair, checking Harry before looking at her curiously. "If you were so nervous about this, I'm surprised you jumped the gun." He checked his watch. "Dinner isn't for a few hours yet."

She took a deep breath and tried to sound nonchalant. "Actually, I came for Harry."

"Harry? What on earth for?" he asked, leveling a thoughtful stare on her. Sharron missed the wariness in his voice as she fidgeted with a piece of torn webbing at the edge of the chair.

"I need to borrow him for just a couple of minutes. And we'll go around the front way now that you've seen me. That wall is murder on the nerves," she muttered, eyeing the stone structure with less trust than she'd have given a cobra.

Griff was frankly surprised. And extraordinarily disappointed. A couple of other women had thought to get past his defenses by making up to Harry—using him to lure Griff into a commitment. It hadn't worked, but that hadn't stopped them from trying.

He hadn't expected this, not from Sharron. Less than twenty-four hours into their affair, she was making a play for Harry. And once she'd made the seemingly unforeseen transition from "childless by choice" to "nurturing mommy," she'd be trying to convince him he'd made the wrong choices about marriage.

He hadn't. The choices he'd made would stand despite her efforts to the contrary.

"So is it okay?" she asked.

"Why do you want him?"

Her moan of distress confused him . . . but that was nothing compared to what he felt at her answer.

"It's the TV," she said, avoiding his stare. "I'm having a problem with it."

"And you want *Harry* to fix it?" Confusion gave way to total bewilderment.

"It's not exactly broken," she said, swallowing the last of her pride. "But there are a few things I need to know that Harry seems to understand."

"Like—?"

"How to turn it on." There. It was out. The humiliating truth. Ignoring the sudden burst of laughter from the adjoining chair, she followed Harry's swooping form with her eyes. This was what she'd been afraid of, what she'd tried to avoid. It was bad enough being the only person she knew who still considered personal computers a passing fad. Now she'd had to confess to being a total misfit in the electronic age.

An eternity later, the laughter subsided. Griff reached across the gap between them for her hand, but she yanked it away in a moment of justifiable pique.

He settled for patting her knee. "Why ask Harry instead of me?"

"I had the impression it would be somewhat less embarrassing." The underlying reprimand was deadly enough to squash bugs. But Griff wasn't a bug. Nor was he suitably squashed.

"New TV?" he asked, the laughter catching at his words.

"New everything," she said, finally getting up the nerve to look him in the eye. "And I wasn't there when they installed it."

"What about reading the manual?"

"Japanese and German."

"Why not call the guys who set it up?" With one finger, he traced a lazy path down the bare skin of her arm to the inside of her elbow. She was particularly sensitive there, he remembered, and soft. He circled the small depression with deliberate precision, and was rewarded with a shudder she couldn't tame.

She took several small, quick breaths before answering. "I meant to call, but I kept forgetting. Besides, I wasn't thrilled about having anyone know how dense I am about these things. Repairmen can be so darned condescending," she added, glaring at him as if to include him in that category.

"And you didn't particularly care what Harry thought?"

"I think I can live with the humiliation of Harry knowing I'm an electronic lightweight." Her gaze turned frankly scolding. "In any case, I'm sure he'll be much more understanding than you've been."

"Perhaps." Griff relaxed, reassured that her intentions were no less than she'd stated. He felt a bit guilty, though, because Sharron had not once indicated she saw Harry as anything more than a child. Not a pawn or a lever, but simply a child.

A child she was becoming attached to. A woman who didn't like children wouldn't have rolled in the garden with one.

A woman who didn't care wouldn't have bought comics and crayons for a sick child. She wouldn't have talked with the toddler on the phone during the quiet times, sharing news of her day and listening with incredible patience to a three-year-old's accounting of his.

Yes, Griff could see the affection she felt for Harry even if Sharron didn't . . . and he realized her maternal instincts weren't entirely absent from her makeup after all.

They were only a little buried beneath claims of selfishness, independence, and just plain ignorance. She'd convinced herself using these excuses, but Griff was no longer fooled.

He knew, then, that it would give him incredible satisfaction if he could teach her the truth she hid from herself. If he could do that, then perhaps when it was time for them to go their separate ways, he could think of her and know he'd helped her find the joy that only children could bring to one life's.

There was no danger in things getting complicated, he decided. Sharron was honorable and would never consider amending the conditions of their arrangement so long as she believed he never intended to marry.

He got up from the chair and pulled her up to walk

beside him. "You can borrow Harry, but you've got to do me a little favor."

Sharron scowled and wondered if she'd have been better off with the technicians. "What favor?"

"Keep him over there long enough for me to run a few miles. I need the exercise." He dropped her hand as they neared the swings.

"Thirty minutes?" She figured she could keep Harry from tearing up her house for that long.

"Forty-five. I'll pick him up when I'm done." Grabbing the seat of Harry's swing midflight, he held his son aloft with teasing threats of dropping, turning him upside down, and other mayhem. In the end, he let the swing go to the accompaniment of Harry's high-pitched screams of delight.

Sharron barely managed not to yell at them both for taking such stupid chances, only grudgingly admitting to herself Griff was stronger than she and therefore in better control of the situation than she could possibly imagine.

It didn't make it any easier to watch.

"Forty-five minutes and not a second more," she said, wincing as Griff all but launched Harry into the trees.

"Deal."

Griff held the tall glass under the faucet for a third time before he shut off the cold water.

Sharron reached into the freezer for another ice cube and plopped it into his glass. "Seems to me all that exercise might be counterproductive. You look like you need a long winter's rest."

"Just because I was a little winded when I walked in here—"

"Stumbled."

He acknowledged the point with a glare. "I haven't been running since we moved here. Without anyone to watch Harry, I can't get out when I need to. It's normal to get a little out of shape if you don't keep up a regular schedule."

"As long as *you're* convinced," she said skeptically, even as her gaze roved with fascination over the smooth, tanned skin revealed by the sleeveless tank top he wore over nylon running shorts. She could almost feel the softness of all that bare flesh, the steel and heat just beneath it. Sweat coated the muscles and the hollows that stretched between, giving off the not unpleasant tang of a man who had pushed himself to the limits of his strength.

Her body stirred in response to his compelling masculinity.

Griff watched her face as she studied him, idly musing that sophistication was vastly overrated if it meant Sharron would be able to hide her thoughts and emotions from him. He couldn't imagine missing the look on her face as she visually discovered his body—and found it to her liking.

All the years of sweating to keep his body in some sort of reasonable shape were suddenly worth it.

"I like how you look at me, honey," he murmured, putting down the glass and leaning against the counter.

"The honesty of your expressions is one of the most erotic things about you."

She looked into his face and blinked rapidly as though awakening from a trance. "I wasn't staring—"

He laughed. "Yes, you were."

She gulped and glanced away. "I'll just look in on Harry."

"Me too."

She shot him a hard look. "Just don't sit on anything."

Griff looked down at his shirt that was ringed in sweat and decided not to be offended. Reaching across her shoulder, he pushed open the swinging door and followed her into the living room.

"Hi, Dad." Harry waved without taking his eyes off the television.

Griff said hi, then asked Sharron how the lesson had gone.

"Piece o' cake," she said. "As long as I remember which remote to use for video and which for plain TV, I should be okay." She hoped she didn't sound as dubious as she felt. Harry's explanation of which remote was which had been filled with exceptions to the simple instruction and additional explanations for complicated gambits that sounded so extravagant, Sharron felt she'd wandered onto the set of *Star Trek* again.

She'd made him go back to step one and repeat it several times before letting him off the hook.

"And Harry didn't make you crazy?"

She followed his gaze to the fragile figurines on the

coffee table just a few feet from where Harry sat. "I decided to try your method."

A raised brow was his only response.

"I walked him through the house and told him what not to touch. It appears to have worked."

"Amazing what kids are capable of learning, isn't it?" Griff didn't think she need look so surprised. "Out of curiosity, is there anything he *is* allowed to touch?"

The doorbell interrupted her reply. Sharron had to be satisfied with a quick glare into his laughing eyes before turning away. She opened the door to a plump, middle-aged woman who gave her a congenial smile.

"I've come for Harry, dear. Is he ready?"

"Who?" Sharron wasn't used to finding someone on her doorstep who had come to see anyone besides herself. It threw her off balance.

The woman looked disconcerted. "Harry Ross." She stepped back and checked the number on the house. "He's about so tall," she said, gesturing about hop high. "Blond, wears funny clothes."

"Oh. *That* Harry." Sharron wondered how she'd known he was there.

"Mr. Ross said he'd be here." The woman shot her a suspicious glance and tried to get a peek inside. "What have you done with him?"

"He's right here, Mrs. Claymore." Griff touched Sharron's shoulder, urging her to stand aside. Harry stood beside his father, smiling up at the adults as Griff smiled at Mrs. Claymore. The older woman beamed back at him, clearly not at all bothered by all the bare skin and sweat.

Sharron smiled because she didn't want to feel left out.

"I'll pick him up about four. Is that all right?" Griff asked, bending down to kiss Harry's cheek.

Mrs. Claymore nodded, holding her hand out to the child. "Anytime, Mr. Ross. I have two others coming to play this afternoon. We'll have a lovely time."

"Bye, Shawon." Harry took the outstretched hand with no hesitation, recalling to Sharron's mind how easily he went with strangers.

"Bye, Harry. Thanks for the lesson." She didn't like the idea of Harry going off with someone she didn't know.

"No sweat. Bye, Dad."

"See you later, Sport. Have fun."

Sharron watched with genuine uneasiness as Harry went with Mrs. Claymore to the car at the curb. When he turned to wave, Sharron lifted a hand in response.

"Who is she?" She tried to get a look at the car's license plate, but was foiled when Griff pulled her away from the door and shut it.

"Harry's daycare." He leaned against the door and folded his arms across his chest. "While Harry was busy infecting the kids in this town with the pox, I left the moms in charge a couple of times and interviewed a half-dozen people. Mrs. Claymore won."

"What do you know about her?"

"She—"

"Did you check her references?"

"I—"

"How can he just leave like that?" she fumed, totally ignoring Griff. "Doesn't he know he's not supposed to trust people he's never met before?" Sharron paced the short width of the hallway, nibbling her lip as she worked herself into a lather. "It's bad enough that he came to me that day without knowing who I was. But when a total stranger comes to the door—"

"She's not a total stranger, Sharron." Griff clamped his jaw tight to hold back the smile. Couldn't she see how parental she was acting? How nurturing? He kept himself from saying anything, knowing it was too early to talk about it.

When Sharron didn't look any more convinced than before, he added, "Mrs. Claymore came to visit Harry before I made a final decision. I wouldn't have hired her if they hadn't liked each other."

"Oh." His quiet reassurance left her deflated and at a loss to explain why she'd gotten worked up over the matter in the first place. "I guess that's okay then."

He pushed away from the door with his shoulders and came to stand beside her. "I thought Harry would do better getting used to this a little at a time. Half a day instead of a whole one." His hand curved behind her neck where he massaged the tense muscles he found there. "Harry needs to be in daycare about four days a week, depending on my schedule. I think Mrs. Claymore's home-style environment is the best thing I can do for him."

Sharron licked her lips and felt a new kind of tension replace the illogical panic of a few moments before. "So why today? Do you need to get to work?"

Griff nodded, his fingers threading into her hair and

warming her scalp. His smile was warm and tempting, a magnet that drew her up onto her toes. "Yes, honey, I've got to work. But I can spare a couple of minutes if you're really insistent."

"I'm not insisting anything," she whispered, her fingertips resting on his chest for balance. "I could use a few extra hours' practice. I have a small concert in a few weeks . . ."

"A few weeks is a long time. All I'm suggesting is a few minutes . . . relaxation." He brushed her mouth with his, then dragged the tip of his tongue between her lips. "Open your mouth, honey. Show me how you like me to kiss you."

She opened for him with a sigh that he swallowed as his mouth fitted over hers. His tongue slid across hers in a rasping caress that made her open wider, demanding more. Her palms inched up his shoulders where the sheen of sweat made his smooth skin slippery and pliant to her touch. He made love to her mouth with a thoroughness that sent shivers coursing through her.

Griff felt her begin to lean toward him, and as much as he would have liked her soft curves rubbing against him, he tangled his hands in her hair and gently tugged. She stared up at him, confusion clouding her eyes.

He swallowed over a harsh groan. "Just let me kiss you, honey. I'm too sweaty for anything else." He urged her head back even farther to expose her long, creamy neck. His mouth traced a line from her chin downward, finding the delicate pulse and teasing it with the tip of his tongue. Then he returned to her mouth because it was the closest he could get to being inside her.

She pulled against his restraining hold, forcing him to soften his control or hurt her. She melted against him, defying him with her body to pull her away again.

He couldn't. He felt the shuddering of her breasts through the thin layers of cloth between them, her bare legs grazing his. His hips rocked toward her, and he was on the point of cupping her fanny with his hands and pulling her hard between his legs when he remembered where they were.

And how she'd reacted to his lovemaking last night. She'd had trouble facing him today, unaccustomed to looking into the face of a lover who wasn't really her lover, not totally. She'd been embarrassed and shy, not quite ready to accept the realities of a sexual relationship. He wanted to teach her to enjoy intimacy without stripping her of the shyness he found so adorable.

He wanted her to know that she could trust him to remember the romance. Always.

With a heartfelt groan, he took his last taste from her mouth and stepped back, ignoring with his last scrap of control the sensual surrender he saw in her eyes. "Wear something washable tonight, honey. Harry's planning on helping us make the pizza."

"He cooks too?" she asked, touching her lips with fingers that were not quite steady.

"He's pretty good for a three-year-old." Griff reached back to open the door. "He inherited it from me."

NINE

The pizza was a success, although Sharron was a bit put out when the male contingent banished her to the "watch—don't help" side of the counter before it was half made.

That had been right after she'd tried to put raw sausage on top of the pepperoni. She'd found it in the refrigerator, and was busily throwing it on when Griff turned from cutting the pineapple. He grabbed her wrist and removed her hand from the vicinity of the pizza. "Harry, get over here and pick off this sausage before she poisons us."

Harry turned from cleaning mushrooms and gave her a disgusted look. "If we'd wanted sausage, we would have cooked some."

"But I like sausage on pizza—"

"So do we," Griff said, leading her around the counter and lifting her onto a stool. "But you have to cook it first. Since I was running late, we decided to do without."

"You have to cook it first?" When he nodded, she

made a surprised sound, then shrugged. "I did warn you that I don't know my way around a kitchen."

He shut his eyes and took a deep breath that signaled his total disbelief anyone could be so unschooled in the culinary arts. Still, when he opened his eyes, there was a gentle look there that let her know cooking wasn't critical to their relationship.

He forgave her . . . and didn't let her close to the food the rest of the night.

Or any other time they were together.

During the next week, Sharron got used to spending her free time in twosomes and threesomes. She and Griff ate out a couple of evenings thanks to Mrs. Claymore's granddaughter, who was old enough to baby-sit.

Sharron never wore the fantasy dress, even though they went to restaurants where it would have been appropriate. Griff never asked about it, and she convinced herself that she had too many other things to wear to worry about a little red dress that still had the price tag dangling from it.

They took Harry to McDonald's one night and ate at Griff's the rest of the time. Griff got back into the routine of running every afternoon, bringing Harry to stay with Sharron when he wasn't at Mrs. Claymore's. In return, he mowed her grass—a chore she detested—and dug out a wedge in the corner of the backyard and filled it with gardening soil so she could expand her garden.

All of which caused Harry to demand his own garden, a chore Griff and Sharron shared with the toddler. Griff dug and hauled, Harry planted, and Sharron sat on a chair and told them what to do. Harry and Griff were sweaty, dirty, and exhausted by the time the garden was "just right," according to the director who was as fresh and rested as she'd been at the onset of the project.

It didn't dawn on either of the males until much later that she might possibly be exacting revenge for the pizza incident.

Along with her daily practicing, Sharron began to prepare for the classes she would teach that fall and the handful of concerts she'd agreed to give, all of which were still over two months away. She made a couple of trips to the university, taking Harry with her once because Griff had a meeting and Harry had resisted spending the entire day at Mrs. Claymore's when he'd been there four full days that week already.

She even gave Harry his first piano lessons, and was astonished to discover a willingness to learn. That led Griff to ask—rather gruffly, she thought—if he was supposed to buy Harry a piano now because all Harry could talk about was how much he liked Shawon's.

She laughed and said no, a piano wasn't necessary . . . yet. Give Harry a little time, let him practice on hers. Then, if she really thought he'd maintain his interest, perhaps Griff might rent something suitable.

He didn't have room for a grand piano, he said. Not even a baby grand.

She was thinking of something more along the lines of an upright, but didn't correct him because if Harry were truly interested in music, a good piano wouldn't be a bad investment.

And so went the week. Sharron found herself included in all aspects of Harry and Griff's lives, joining them in everything from baking cookies to bath time. Baking, she was quick to point out, was a skill she'd picked up out of necessity. No one should have to go without homemade chocolate chip cookies, and she amazed and astounded her audience of two with some of the best cookies they'd ever had. As for bath time, Sharron was a sucker for anything that floated, and Harry had an army of things that bobbled, dove, and rocketed from beneath the surface. If Harry had been really good that day—as if he could do anything wrong, she told his father—he was allowed to use his father's spa-sized tub. During the hourlong bath, Sharron managed to get as wet as the child. When Griff pointed this out, she claimed that it was because she was too short to lean over the tub without getting wet. Griff just shook his head as he dried her off, mumbling something about bringing over her swimsuit, before he reached into the tub for the other wet body.

She was so content with her role as friend and playmate that she made herself deliberately ignore the certain knowledge that it wouldn't always be that way.

The one thing she didn't ignore was how Griff touched her. Kissed her. Held her.

He touched her often, reminding her that he was there, close by. Innocent caresses that were more familiar than they were provocative. She grew accustomed to his touch, his presence.

He kissed her a lot too. Soft, gentle kisses that warmed her soul, kisses that explored the friendship between them without touching on the passion. When she opened her mouth for more, for a deeper kiss, he would murmur nonsense that she didn't understand and stop kissing her altogether.

He held her in arms that were strong and comforting, pulling her against his side as they walked down the street, coming up behind her as she watched Harry at play and sliding his arms around her waist. It felt natural to be in his arms, yet he never once pulled her close, never allowed her to rub her tingling body against his.

She was rapidly going out of her mind.

After a week of such torture, Thursday morning found her just a touch moody.

She wanted the intimacies of sex, the excitement of passion she'd tasted in Griff's arms.

Sharron admitted that to herself, then took it a step further and blamed her irritability on frustration. Sexual frustration, she clarified, glad to have a reason for the mood she'd been in from the moment she'd awakened. Checking her watch, she frowned and dug through her drawers for something appropriate for the day's activities. They were going to Marine World, followed by a short tour of San Francisco's Fisherman's Wharf on their way home. She would have just enough time to dress and water her plants if she hurried.

She didn't feel like hurrying.

She felt like going back to bed and telling Griff and Harry to go by themselves. But she couldn't do that.

She'd promised Harry she'd come with them, and his father's restrained caresses and kisses weren't going to ruin her day.

She'd tackle Griff about it that night, demand an explanation for his ridiculous behavior.

She wanted him to make love to her and couldn't imagine what on earth he was waiting for. He knew she was on the pill, just as she knew he'd bought a box of condoms. Even if the pill wasn't yet at its maximum effectiveness, the condoms would certainly do the trick.

Why did she imagine he might make love to her when he wouldn't even kiss her properly?

She would have thought he'd changed his mind about making love to her at all were it not for the handful of times she'd caught him looking at her with so much desire in his expression, she'd nearly fainted under the force of it.

Fainted! The concept was vaguely appealing if it meant Griff would finally take notice of her. She fanned her face, blaming the flare of heat on frustration, then pulled on a sleeveless knit top and white slacks. Determined to put her irritation aside, she hurried through her chores and was waiting with a smile on her face when Griff and Harry knocked at the door.

Together, the three of them piled into Griff's car and set off on an adventure that had Harry babbling with excitement. That was a good thing, because Sharron didn't have the energy to say much of anything.

Sharron put Harry on his feet, then dug into her purse for a tissue and used it to wipe the thin film of perspiration from the back of her neck. Carrying Harry the last hundred yards had worn her down faster than she would have thought possible. Griff had gone ahead to get the car, saying something about Sharron looking too tired to walk the distance. Well, she *was* too tired, but so was Harry, especially after hours of traipsing around the park. So she'd carried him to the entrance, his hot little body draped over hers in his first quiet moment all day, a day that had been filled with adventure. And food. And walking.

She was pooped.

They'd watched the seals, dolphins, and killer whales perform, as well as water-skiers and acrobats. They'd eaten pizza under metal umbrellas, chasing off the bees that swarmed everywhere until it made more sense to put as much distance between themselves and the pizza area as possible.

They'd sat on the bleachers and watched a magic show, then taken Harry to ride the baby elephant. And when they'd tried to distract Harry from noticing the lion and tiger show because they were certain he was wearing out—*they* certainly were—he'd gone all contrary on them and insisted that he wanted to do it all.

He went through the blue whale play area four times

before they convinced him it would still be there another day.

Leaning against a cool wall, Sharron fanned herself with a park map and numbly watched Harry burn off a few hundred calories as he chased around a nearby pillar. The never-ending circles were making her dizzy, but she didn't take her eyes off him because they were in a crowded place, surrounded by strangers.

She'd have given anything to close her eyes and rest. The outing had taken its toll. She wasn't even frustrated with Griff's friendly treatment anymore.

She couldn't think much beyond getting cool.

Griff took one look at Sharron's face as she collapsed in the passenger seat and told her Harry was too tired for Fisherman's Wharf. They'd do it another time, he said, then suggested she relax and enjoy the scenery. They took the long way back, crossing the Oakland Bay Bridge because Harry wanted to go through the long tunnel in the middle, then worked their way through the crowded streets of San Francisco to the Golden Gate Bridge, from which they could see hundreds of white sails in the bay beneath them.

The cool bay air somewhat relieved her exhaustion, and she found the energy to say yes when Griff suggested they stop along the way for an early supper. He pulled off the Redwood Highway at San Anselmo, where they ate at a small diner on the main street of the picturesque town. Afterward, they took Harry to a park just a half block up the street where he frolicked on the grass with such energy that just watching him made her exhaustion return. Griff wiped perspiration from her forehead with his handkerchief and teased her about being so out of shape that she couldn't walk a half block without sweating. It was the heat, she told him. She hated being hot. And besides, they'd walked miles at Marine World.

What she couldn't understand was how Harry was still standing. Griff said something about children not running out of energy until there were chores to do, then pulled her to her feet to walk back to the car.

She fell asleep in the front seat and was oblivious to everything until Griff shook her awake.

"You'll have to exercise more if a little tour of Marine World wipes you out this badly," he said, carrying her purse to the door when she would have left it on the floor of the car.

"I hate exercise," she grumbled, irritated that he looked as though he had enough energy in reserve to run a few miles. "And I was tired before we left. I must not be getting enough sleep."

"You went to bed at nine, honey." A single brow lifted in mocking disbelief. "At least that was what you said you were going to do when you left to go home last night."

"So maybe ten hours' sleep isn't enough," she snapped. "It's not like I have anything better to do with my nights." Her key turned in the lock, and she kicked the door open when it wouldn't give to a gentle push.

Griff glanced over his shoulder to make sure Harry hadn't let himself out of his car seat, then cupped her chin in one big hand. "Are you telling me there's something missing from your nights?"

She all but growled. "I wish you'd quit teasing, Griff. It's making me a bit tense."

"Teasing?" His tone was gently chiding. "I'm not teasing you, Sharron. I just decided to back up a little, to let you know me before we made love. I thought you'd be more at ease with a lover who was also your friend."

"Is that what you've been doing? Trying to make me comfortable so I won't blush every time I look at you?"

He nodded. "You needed time. I was trying to give it to you."

"So explain why I feel so irritable!" she demanded, stepping inside and turning to face him with her arms crossed defensively across her chest. "It's all I can do to keep from punching something." Or someone, she added silently.

"That's not precisely the reaction I was looking for." He thought about it for a moment, then brightened. "Maybe you're frustrated, and that's making you irritable."

"*Of course I'm frustrated!* Is that so difficult to understand?" Her jaw clenched, and she stared balefully at him. "I want you to make love to me, and all I'm getting are friendly little kisses and pats."

Griff grinned broadly, thinking his tactics had worked even better than he'd hoped. A week ago, she wouldn't have dared bring up the subject of making love, not without blushing.

Now, though, she was almost yelling at him. Her face

was flushed with heat, but no more so than it had been for the past few hours.

She wasn't blushing. He was satisfied.

"Would you like me to come over tonight, Sharron?" he asked quietly, thinking to gentle her mood with his own. "We can make love all night long, if you like." His mind scrambled ahead, past baby-sitter to champagne and music. He'd been aching so long to thrust himself inside her, it didn't seem possible it would happen that night.

Then again, maybe not, he mused as she scowled at him. Sharron didn't look like a woman who was going to melt from passion.

"Not even in your dreams, Griff. The only thing I'm going to do tonight is sleep."

"Tomorrow night, then," he said, undaunted by her delay because she was, he admitted, looking more than a bit frayed around the edges.

She scowled again. "We'll see." She thrust her fingers into her hair, sighing heavily because she was tired and irritable and knew she wasn't behaving well.

It was all Griff's fault.

She had to get a grip! With a forced smile, she thanked him for the day out, and said she wouldn't forget she was taking Harry to get his hair cut the following afternoon. It had been her idea, based on the recent discovery that Griff cut his son's hair himself.

Harry deserved better.

Griff set her purse down on a hall table without crossing the doorstep. "Are you going to be all right, honey?"

"I'll be fine. I just need to get a full night's sleep."

"You look like you're coming down with something."

She leveled an admonishing stare on him. "I *never* get sick."

"Oh." He nodded, hiding his grin. "Then it must be the sun that's made you all red."

"I'm fine," she all but shouted. Sighing again, she caught her long hair in her hands and lifted if from her neck just in case there was a breeze around. There wasn't, and that irritated her too.

He kissed her lightly and told her to go right to bed—as if she had anything else on her mind, she thought crossly. Still, she managed to nod and summon up a smile, albeit a strained one.

"Good night, then," Griff said. "I'll call you in the morning." He'd hardly gotten the words out when she muttered good night and slammed the door.

Frowning with concern, Griff walked back to the parked car. It was more than exhaustion, he guessed. A cold, perhaps. She looked a touch feverish. Sliding behind the wheel, he decided he'd come over and check on her first thing in the morning.

Obviously, getting sick wasn't something Sharron did without a fight, he mused, a smile curving his lips as he recalled her rapidly escalating irritation.

A week ago, she wouldn't have been relaxed enough with him to let her cranky side show. Today, however, his reaction to her mood was a low priority.

And on top of it all, she thought she was irritable out of frustration. He figured she was only half right. Frustration on top of getting a cold or whatever. He didn't like the idea of her being sick. It filled him with the same kind of helplessness he felt when Harry was ill.

He didn't mind that she was frustrated, though. Once she felt better, he'd take care of easing that problem . . . for them both.

He wasn't even particularly bothered at having the door slammed in his face, although he did hope his son hadn't noticed. Harry had once slammed his bedroom door in a fit of temper. Griff's solution had been simple. He'd calmly unscrewed the door from its hinges and left it off for a week to teach his son that doors were for privacy and not for slamming.

The tactic had worked because Harry hadn't slammed a door on purpose since.

Griff did a U-turn and headed back down the street toward home, thinking he'd call her late in the morning, because if she did indeed have a cold, a long, uninterrupted sleep was the best remedy.

"Dad?"

"Hmm?"

"Do I get to help you take off Shawon's door?"

TEN

Thanks to an unscheduled meeting with a nervous client who needed to be reassured his plans were being drawn in accordance with his specifications, Griff didn't get around to calling Sharron until noon.

A night's sleep hadn't improved her mood. When she finally picked up the phone after the twelfth ring, she mumbled something about it being incredibly impolite to wake a person at the crack of dawn, then hung up before he could inquire what time the sun rose at her end of the block.

Five minutes later, he was pounding on her front door. When she didn't come, he tried the knob. The door was unlocked. Griff filed away her carelessness for future reference and let himself in, nearly tripping over her shoes that she'd left in the entryway. The house was quiet and stuffy, and he frowned as he realized she hadn't bothered opening any windows before going to bed. Sharron was a fresh-air freak, she'd admitted to him during one of their late-night telephone sessions. She couldn't sleep in a room that was closed up.

His concern magnified. Griff headed down the corridor to her room with a sinking feeling in the pit of his stomach, calling out her name so that he wouldn't frighten her.

That wasn't even an issue. He found her in bed, sound asleep and clearly oblivious to the fact that she was no longer alone in the house. She was sprawled on her back, the bedcovers a snarled confusion that only half covered her and revealed to Griff that she'd slept in panties and a camisole. Her slacks and blouse littered a trail from doorway to bed, and the ribbon she'd worn in her hair was tangled in with the sheets.

The flush of fever was obvious on her face and chest, but it was the half-dozen patches of angry, red rash that made him suck in his breath. Chicken pox.

He began to feel a little sick himself.

Griff hesitated at the side of the bed and wondered how he was going to wake her without scaring her half to death, then he realized that waking her up was premature. First, he needed to call her doctor.

Turning on his heels, he retraced his steps to the front door, then went into the kitchen where he remembered seeing her personal phone book. He said a word of thanks that she'd written in the name of her doctor on a page with all the other emergency numbers and information. Griff dialed the number listed for Brent Lawrence, MD.

Five minutes later, he hung up the phone and headed back to the bedroom, where he searched in her dresser drawers until he found a relatively modest cotton nightgown. Turning, he eyed the woman on the bed and wondered how he was going to get her into the nightgown without waking her.

He didn't. He'd no sooner begun to pull the camisole up across her breasts when her eyes flew open and she said, "I'm not in the mood, Griff."

He grinned. "I know, honey. I'm only trying to get you more comfortable." He showed her the cotton gown, but she just sniffed at it and tugged the camisole back down to cover her breasts.

"I was asleep," she said. "Why do you keep waking me up when you know I don't want to get up this early?"

"It's afternoon, Sharron," he said, easing down beside her thighs. "If you want the doctor to examine you in your undies instead of a gown, that's your choice. Not that it really makes any difference, though, because I imagine he'll want to see—"

"What doctor?" she demanded crossly. "I didn't call a doctor."

"I did." He dared to touch the side of her face. When she didn't bite his hand off, he caressed her with deliberate, calming strokes, "You're sick, honey. That's why I called the doctor."

"Doctors don't make house calls."

"When I described your symptoms, your doctor decided he'd better come on over to see for himself." He deliberately left out what there was to be seen.

"It's a waste of time."

"Why don't we let Dr. Lawrence decide that for himself?"

She tugged at the sheet until a corner of it partially covered her torso, then rubbed her palm across her forehead. "I feel lousy," she conceded.

"So you don't mind that I called the doctor?"

"I probably have a cold, Griff," she said, emphasizing *cold* as if it deserved less mention than a bug bite. "Or the flu perhaps. I never could tell the two apart." Her eyelids drifted closed, then opened halfway as she leveled a decidedly mocking gaze on him. "You're going to feel pretty stupid when the doctor yells at you for dragging him all the way across town just to diagnose a simple . . . cold."

Griff decided to let the doctor tell her the news.

Sighing, he picked up the nightgown and held it in front of her face. "So what's it going to be, Shar? Undies or a gown?"

Obviously, the thought of his comeuppance had sweetened her temper, because she took the gown and told him to turn his back while she changed into it.

"Griff?" she said, a couple of minutes later as he straightened the sheets and tucked them neatly around her.

"Hmm?"

"Did you happen to notice that I've been a little cranky lately?"

He handed her a glass of water he'd brought from the bathroom. "I noticed."

"I'm surprised you're putting up with it."

"Everyone gets irritable once in a while, Sharron.

What's the point of getting to know each other if you only stick around for good moods and laughter?" He tidied up the bedroom as he talked, willing her to understand that he wanted to know all of her, not just the surface person. "Besides, you're cute when you're cranky."

"I slammed the door in your face." She swallowed all the water and set it aside. "That's definitely not cute."

He told her what Harry had to say about slamming doors. She actually grinned when he then threatened dire circumstances if she ever slammed another door again.

He was only giving her a second chance because he knew she didn't feel well, he said. He'd told Harry the same thing, although she could expect a stern lecture from his son on the merits of privacy.

Griff eased down on the bed and took her hand, threading his fingers through hers. "It's all right if you get mad at me, Shar. Heaven knows Harry and I have falling-outs more days than not."

"I'm not angry with you, though," she said. "It's not like you've done anything wrong."

"Except not kiss you like you wanted," he murmured, holding her hand against his chest. "Not hold you like you needed to be held, not make love with you even though we were both dying inside at the wait."

She nodded, the brief flare of a blush deepening her color. "I admit I was a touch upset with you over that. It didn't occur to me I might be sick too. I *never* get sick."

He grinned. "I remember you saying something to that effect yesterday."

"I thought I was just frustrated." She held his gaze

with her own, defying him to look away as her color heightened. "I can't believe I said that!"

"Twice. You mentioned it yesterday too."

"How could I forget?" She swallowed hard and tightened her fingers around his. "I wouldn't have said that a week ago."

"Which means you're comfortable with me now."

"And frustrated."

His laugh was low and warm. "I know, honey. We'll fix that as soon as you're up to it."

"Promise?"

He promised. "You concentrate on getting well first."

She seemed satisfied, then, because her whole body relaxed in a way it hadn't since she'd awakened. Her eyes drifted closed, and she tucked his hand beside her cheek.

Griff sat at her side and stroked her hair back from her forehead as he tried to ignore the rash blossoming on her arms.

He prayed the doctor would arrive before she started to itch.

"Chicken pox!"

Griff heard her shout all the way in the living room. She'd banished him from her room upon the doctor's arrival, an exile Griff had been only too willing to accept. If a cold made Sharron cranky, then chicken pox was going to boil her blood.

He supposed he should have warned the doctor that his patient thought she had a cold. But he'd been a little taken aback to discover Sharron's physician was young, good-looking, and not wearing a wedding ring.

Griff wondered how long it would be before he couldn't look at any man without imagining this might be the one she chose to spend the rest of her life with.

Dr. Lawrence appeared around the corner and asked Griff if he would mind coming back to the bedroom. He minded, but he went anyway, not looking forward to facing Sharron.

One of life's real surprises made him hesitate just inside the door. Sharron was lying propped against a mound of pillows, her arms stained with streaks of calamine and the sweetest smile he'd ever seen on her face.

Obviously, the decision to let the doctor break the news had been a good one.

"Starting to itch now?" he asked.

"A little." She lifted a hand to scratch her arm, but lowered it under his warning glare.

"Incubation is twelve to sixteen days," the doctor said, giving her the bottle of calamine to hold to keep her fingers busy. "Sharron says your son must have infected her."

"Harry sneezed on me," she confirmed, patting the bed and waiting until Griff had sat down beside her. The doctor leaned against the wall, his tall, muscular frame relaxed as he watched them with an air of amused tolerance. "When I was drying him after our bout of mud wrestling, he sneezed twice. That must be how I got it."

Griff couldn't figure out why she seemed so damned

pleased about it. "I vaguely remember your being disgusted when I told you how chicken pox was spread."

"Your memory is faulty, Griff," she said with a straight look on her face. "Harry would never do anything disgusting."

"Sneezing all over someone isn't disgusting?"

She just yawned and ignored his rebuttal.

Now he understood. Sharron was delirious. Griff looked at the doctor. "She's obviously out of her mind. Is there anything you can do?"

Lawrence grinned. "I gave her some Tylenol, and her fever is already beginning to subside. I doubt she's so much delirious as she is relieved to find out what's wrong. Apparently, she's been feeling off-key for a couple days and was concerned something else might be wrong."

Griff turned to her. "What?" His gaze narrowed at her wry expression.

"I thought all that frustration was making me ill."

He felt blood heat his face as he stole a glance at the doctor, who appeared to be about to swallow his tongue. Griff stared at Sharron, shaking his head in disbelief. "I can't believe it."

"That I thought I was getting sick because you were frustrating me so badly?" she asked.

"No, dammit. I can't believe you'd actually tell the doctor—"

"People are supposed to tell their doctors everything, Griff," she said. Her smile would have won any competition for innocence. "And considering Brent did prescribe my birth-control pills, I thought—"

"I've already heard what you thought." Griff dropped his chin against his chest and groaned. "And to think I imagined you were such a shy little thing."

Brent, as she'd called him, cleared his throat and pushed himself away from the wall. "As interesting as this might be the second time around, I need to get back to the office." He told Griff to get more calamine lotion and to call if Sharron's fever went back up. Or if she got a severe headache. Or vomited. Or a miscellany of other symptoms Griff had read about in the child-care medical book when caring for Harry. That's what had prompted him to call the doctor in the first place, what he'd read about adults contracting the disease and how hard it could be on them.

Lawrence also cautioned them against having sex for the duration of the disease, because a pregnancy at this time might result in birth defects. Precautions weren't guarantees, he reminded them. Besides, he doubted Sharron was going to feel up to it in any case.

Neither of them blushed at the frank warning, both too relieved that they didn't have that worry clouding their hearts.

When Griff walked the doctor to the door, he assured him he'd be taking Sharron home where he could keep an eye on her. Heading back down the hall, he hoped she wouldn't get all cranky again when he told her about her impending move.

He breathed a sigh of relief to find she was still smiling. It was a good sign.

"I've got the pox, Griff," she said, mischief lighting her eyes.

"Yeah, honey, you've got the pox. Now let me tell you what we're going to do about it."

She didn't give him a single argument about moving to his place, except to warn him she might not always be as easy to get around as she was now.

He said that if she didn't mind him, he'd dress her in footie pajamas and treat her just as he'd treated Harry.

She didn't have any pajamas with feet in them, she pointed out. "In fact, I don't have any pajamas at all. I wear nightgowns."

He leaned down until their noses were almost touching. "And when you're sleeping with me, you won't wear anything at all."

"After I get well," she murmured, a different kind of heat flaring between her thighs.

"After you get well," he agreed, and sealed their bargain with a kiss.

The rash spread across Sharron's arms and legs before nightfall. Ensconced in the guest bedroom that was located right next to Griff's, she quickly lost her sense of humor as Harry and Griff took turns making sure she didn't scratch anywhere near a red spot. If anything, Harry was worse than his father, sitting on her hand once when she refused to obey his directive not to scratch.

She hated chicken pox.

For eight days, Sharron alternately soaked in cool soda baths and coated her skin in the drippy, messy calamine. She thought it was sweet when Griff lay down beside her the first night, thinking he was doing it to comfort her. When she discovered he intended only to ensure she didn't scratch where she itched, she changed her mind.

After a full night during which Griff held her hands away from her body and argued—endlessly!—the merits of not scratching, she learned just how stubborn he could be. The following morning, he went out and scoured the town until he found a pair of footie pajamas that fit her. When she demanded to know where on earth he'd found them, he refused to answer, going as far as to cut the tag from the collar. So that it wouldn't irritate her tender skin, he said.

Sharron was pretty sure he'd been to one of those sexy lingerie shops, but couldn't prove it. She did, however, wonder aloud if his taste in women's sleepwear was always so restrained.

He filled her ears with erotic promises that set her heart beating in that peculiar rhythm only he could impose, then he fixed her a soda bath before seeking a cold shower for himself.

Griff made her wear the pajamas that night so he could get some rest. When he finally fell asleep, Sharron used the muted hum of the fan to disguise the sound of the zipper as she worked it down. He caught her before her arm was half out of the sleeve.

The following night he wired the zipper shut, prying it open again only for necessary intervals.

She hated chicken pox, and she wasn't too pleased with Griff, either.

By the third night, the routine was firmly established.

Griff put Harry to bed, took Sharron to his office where he worked for several hours, then put Sharron to bed. To say they were sleeping together would be stretching the facts. True, they slept, although it was in fits and starts. And yes, they touched in their sleep, although it was generally Griff holding her hands and Sharron edging toward his warmth in the early morning hours. On the chance that Harry might wander in, Griff slept in his clothes—trousers or shorts, stripping off his shirt on the warmer nights.

Still, Sharron knew she was quickly becoming accustomed to having Griff near her at night.

She wondered how she'd ever learn to sleep without him.

Her fever faded entirely after the first couple of days, and none of the other warning symptoms surfaced. The spots were confined to her limbs and stomach, and although she knew how much worse it could have been, she was plenty miserable as it was.

Between Harry and Griff, she was entertained, fed, and reminded—constantly!—not to scratch. Harry had his father install a television in her room, to which they connected his Nintendo machine. As far as distractions went, this was her favorite, although Sharron was miffed that a three-year-old could still beat her even after she'd had nearly a week's practice.

She beat Harry at Chinese checkers, though, a victory that soothed her ego until she discovered he'd never learned to play. All he'd done was imitate her moves, he confessed.

So she taught him to play, then harrangued Griff for not doing it sooner.

Griff was philosophic. "He's only three, Sharron. There's time yet."

"Halfway to four years old, Griffen Ross, and a very bright child he is. By this time next year, he'll be learning to play chess." When she found out Griff didn't play chess, she offered to teach Harry herself.

Tomorrow.

Griff let her do anything she wanted as long as it kept her from scratching.

When she insisted Griff spend more time working, he moved her to the sofa in his office and worked with one eye on his desk and the other on her.

So much for that tactic, she mused, then decided she should be grateful he let her go to the bathroom without monitoring that too. He let her take her baths in peace, but she realized early on that he only did that because the soothing soda water kept her from scratching just as effectively as he did.

Harry smeared her arms and legs with calamine at least a dozen times a day, claiming it as his job. He would have insisted on doing her stomach, too, but Griff intervened and told Harry that Sharron could reach her stomach just fine.

Griff offered to do her stomach, too, but Sharron was adamant about keeping that task for herself. Gathering her in his arms, he teased her about how her shyness was something that shouldn't come between them.

"How could a person be shy after all we've gone through together?" she complained.

"Things have been a bit practical around here," he admitted. "I promise not to think any lewd thoughts if you'll let me do your stomach."

She sighed and shook her head. "I don't think I can let you touch me, intimately, and not want to make love with you." To prove her point, she rested her head on his thigh and felt the muscles bunch in reaction. It reassured her to know he still reacted to her. "See what I mean, Griff. You do the same thing to me."

He cupped her chin so that she was looking into his eyes. "I can't look at you without wanting to make love, Shar."

"I hate having you see me like this," she whispered. "The spots are so ugly—"

"You're beautiful, honey," he murmured against her hair, moving her hand from his thigh before he went out of his mind. "That's why I've been trying to keep you from scratching. I'd hate to see scars on that gorgeous skin of yours, not if we can prevent them."

"So that's why you're so fanatic about it." She yawned, curling into his body as sleep nudged at her consciousness. "And here I thought you were merely being ornery."

She accused him of just that the following afternoon when he caught her scratching the bottom of her foot. "What do you care if I get a scar on my foot?" she demanded.

Griff just sighed and made her put the jammies back on, even though it was midday.

By the time the chicken pox had run its course after eight very long days, everyone was good and fed up with it. Including Harry, who said he was glad he'd got it over with before he was as old as Shawon.

That made her feel just peachy.

When she was no longer contagious, Sharron insisted she could finish recuperating at home.

"It's time, Griff. There's nothing left to scratch, and I'm sure you need to get your own life back in order. I know I've got a lot to catch up on." *I've got to get out of here!* she screamed silently. *Let me go before I fall apart*. She pasted a convincing smile on her face and kept her desperate thoughts to herself as she bustled around the guest room in a flurry of activity that was designed to show Griff she was more than capable of taking care of herself.

"Sure you don't want to stick around here and let Harry and me pamper you for a few more days?" he asked, stilling her frantic movements with a gentle touch.

"I'm sure, Griff. All I have to do is wait for the spots to fade. I'm fine otherwise." *Except my heart, of course, but it's too late to worry about that*. She planted a noisy kiss on his chin and began throwing her odds and ends into her carryall. "When Harry comes home from Mrs. Claymore's, tell him I passed the sixth level on the Nintendo game."

"Why don't you wait and tell him yourself?"

"Because I want to go home now," she said more sharply than she intended, then gave him a conciliatory smile. "I should probably get settled over there before I wear out. That's all." She'd made the decision to leave the moment she'd awakened to Griff's tender smile and Harry's squeals of excitement. It had become a tradition, waking with the Ross males as her first sights and sounds.

It was a tradition that couldn't possibly last. The pain of that realization was what motivated her sudden decision to leave.

Griff finally agreed, but only because he recognized she must need her privacy after her unexpected immersion in an all-male household. He took her back to her house, making a side trip to the grocery store to fill her refrigerator because he knew she wouldn't go out in public until the spots had completely faded.

The house felt quiet and still when she walked inside, and she stood in the hallway as Griff moved through the rooms opening windows.

"I'll bring over dinner tonight, honey," he said, stashing the grocery bags under the sink. "Think you'd like some spaghetti? Harry and I have been wanting to try a new recipe we found in the paper."

Is dinner really a good idea, Griff? Wouldn't it be easier if you just walked out of my life and let me learn to live without you?

"Sounds lovely," she said from behind clenched teeth. "Why don't we eat early so Harry doesn't fall asleep at the table." She stood with her hand on the front door and hoped she didn't look too anxious.

When she thought he was going to walk past her and out the door, he covered her mouth with a searing kiss that was substantially more involved than any they'd shared over the past several days. He filled her ears with whispers of the magic they'd make between them when she was completely well.

What would happen if you knew I'd fallen in love with you, Griff? Would you still make love to me? She returned his kisses, keeping her eyes closed so that he wouldn't see the questions there.

Five days, he told her. Then he kissed her again and made her promise to spend the afternoon napping. She backed against the wall to keep from leaning into his warmth.

I never promised not to love you. Is there a reason you didn't ask that of me?

She told him she'd nap, but only to get him out of the house before the tears began to fall. The fragile control she'd exerted for the last few hours shattered the moment he pulled the door closed behind him. Tears rolled down her cheeks as she slid down the wall and buried her face in arms that were wrapped around her knees.

She was in love with a man who would never love her in return.

Even worse, she was in love with his son.

The thought of living without either of them was more than she could handle. Sharron cried until the tears would come no more, then picked herself up from the floor and went to her bedroom for the nap she'd promised Griff she'd take.

Upon waking several hours later, she knew what she had to do. It was the only thing she *could* do.

Nothing.

Because nothing had changed. At least, nothing that they needed to know about. She loved Griff, and Harry too. She was involved with both of them, on more than one level. If she kept this knowledge to herself, everything would go on as planned.

She and Griff would become lovers, share the erotic secrets they'd only talked about, explore the stars and find pleasure in the journey.

She and Harry would continue their friendship. She would teach him more about music, he would give her lessons in Nintendo. She would watch the world through the eyes of a three-year-old and learn through him what it was like to believe in fairy tales.

If she took the coward's way out and called an end to it all today, her heart would be no less broken than it would be weeks or months down the road.

Sharron picked up the phone and told Griff she was hungry. Then she went into the shower and willed the spots to disappear because five days seemed like an eternity.

Griff and Harry were there almost before she was dry, bringing not only dinner, but also the mail that had been piling up at her postbox. Sharron fell upon it with the glee of a person who loved getting letters, then winced when she came across a reminder for a conference she'd planned to attend in Los Angeles.

"I'll have to go," she told Griff that night after he'd

put Harry to sleep in her bed. "I'm scheduled to speak at one of the workshops."

"When?" He lifted his feet to the coffee table, taking care not to get too close to the fragile crystal collection. When she said in six days, he grumbled that she wouldn't be well by then.

"If I'm well enough to make love with you five days from now, I should certainly be able to take a plane trip south," she pointed out, and was knocked breathless by the heated look of passion in his eyes.

"Remind me again why we're waiting," he said softly, then cupped her chin to bring her mouth to his. He nibbled gently, brushing across her lips as she tried to focus on the reasons they'd decided to wait.

It wasn't easy. "The spots," she reminded him. "I want them to go away—"

"We'll make love in the dark."

She took a deep breath, shaking her head as she backed away from his hungry mouth. Love, she realized, had knocked the shyness right out of her because she couldn't remember ever being this comfortable with him . . . and saying what she was about to say. "We'll make love in the light, Griff. I want to see you."

He groaned and turned his face into the sofa cushion, muttering something about smart-mouthed women whose mission in life was to drive their men wild.

Not long afterward, he was still muttering dark words as he carried a sleeping Harry out of the house.

Griff complained and teased and tested her for five long days, wooing her with a delicate intensity that left her heart beating that special rhythm only he could provoke. Five days during which she saw nearly as much of the two of them as she had when she was living at their house. Five days in which the reminders of the disease faded from her body and she regained her strength.

Five days during which she learned to hide the love.

It wasn't going to happen. Sharron stared at her reflection and knew there was love there that even a blind man could see.

Perhaps it was for the best that Griff wasn't here to see it.

She pulled a suitcase from the top shelf of her closet and set it at the foot of her bed as she thought about Griff's call the day before. His parents had flown in unexpectedly, and he and Harry had gone to San Francisco to spend the night with them in an airport hotel, because there wasn't time to bring them all the way back.

He'd apologized profusely for missing their planned evening together, a hurried apology because there hadn't been much time in between picking up Harry from Mrs. Claymore's and heading into San Francisco.

She'd hated herself for the relief she'd felt at the cancellation of their evening. Postponement, she amended. After Los Angeles.

By agreeing to wait until she was physically ready, they'd essentially put a timetable on their first complete sexual encounter. It made her just a touch nervous. She likened it to pulling a tooth: She just wanted to get it over so they could relax again.

Be friends, as well as lovers.

The doorbell rang as she was trying to decide how many dresses she'd need for the week in Los Angeles. Five or six, she decided as she walked toward the front door. Nothing fancy; sedate worked better in that environment, she knew.

She opened the door to a sweating, speechless man. "Out torturing yourself again, are you?" she asked, her light teasing covering the sudden dryness in her mouth. Griff hadn't said he'd be back before she left for Los Angeles.

She'd thought she wouldn't see him for another week.

He pushed past her and made his way into the kitchen where he found a glass and held it under the tap. "Haven't had time to run since you got sick." He took a long drink, then poured more as he gave her a sidelong stare. "I did eight miles."

"Eight? I thought you said four miles were enough to keep you in shape."

Griff drank two more glasses of water before shutting off the tap. "I did eight so I wouldn't scare you."

She blinked, taking in the sweat-stained shorts and shirt, heaving chest, and oxygen-inflated muscles in his thighs. "It didn't work, Griff," she said, swallowing back something that was less fear than excitement. "I think you're scaring me."

He shook his head and set down the glass. Walking toward her, he raked his gaze over her short skirt and sleeveless top. "I've been wanting you for so long, I knew it would happen too fast. So I ran, tried to knock back my libido to something I can control." He reached out a hand and rested it on her shoulder.

"Do you think it worked?" she whispered.

His smile was slow and entirely male. He didn't answer, but said instead, "What do you have planned for this afternoon, honey?"

"I have to pack."

He bent his head to brush his lips across hers, and she rested her fingertips against his chest for balance. "I'll help," he murmured, then threaded his fingers into her hair and pulled her head back. He trailed kisses across her face, along her cheeks, her eyelids, her jaw.

"I have . . . to be . . . at the airport . . . by six." Her hands slid up his shoulders, the sheen of his sweat a familiar sensation, a warmth she reveled in.

"I have to pick up Harry at four." He pushed aside the collar of her blouse and nibbled on the exposed skin. One hand slid up her arm to capture her wrist. He turned it so he could see the dial of her watch. "That gives us three hours, honey."

"Three hours," she echoed, engrossed in the feel of his skin beneath her fingers. So smooth, she marveled. And hard, although it seemed a contradiction that he could be both.

He stepped back, holding her face captive with the gentle pressure of his fingers. There was a flicker of mischief in his eyes that she'd never seen before.

And a flare of passion that she had.

"What do you say, Shar? Do you really want to go to Los Angeles without knowing what it's like to feel me come inside you?" He cocked his head at the heat that bloomed in her cheeks, his gaze narrowing on hers as he gave her time to think about it. "I know that it would please me very much to make love with you this afternoon."

She stared helplessly up at him and knew he had his answer when he smiled and let out a long, harsh breath. Still silent, she watched as he turned from her and strode down the hall toward her bedroom. Warring factions of apprehension and excitement kept her rooted to the spot long after he had disappeared.

He was waiting for her, in her room. Waiting to make love, to take them both to the stars.

Sharron drew in a deep shuddering breath, then another. Her body tingled with the anticipation of what awaited her just a few feet away, yet the shyness that was so deeply ingrained in her being made her hesitate.

They would be making love in daylight, just as she'd requested. Hoped.

She would be able to watch as she touched him, see his response.

She smiled and knew that the shyness had finally gone. Maybe.

It was her own laughter that she heard as she hurried down the hall to meet a lover who knew her at least as well as she knew herself.

A man whom she would love with her last dying breath.

ELEVEN

She found him in the bathroom.

Drawn by the sound of the shower, Sharron passed through the door he'd left ajar, pausing only to kick off her shoes. Griff shut off the water and slid open the door as she hesitated somewhere between desire and the infinitely more familiar shyness.

It hadn't gone away after all.

Shyness achieved a marginal victory, bonding her to the cold tiles as she studied with great interest the wallpaper beyond his left shoulder. Her heart thudded in her chest, and she barely managed to keep from squeezing her eyes shut. Fisting her hands in her skirt, she wished for the nerve to make the first move.

She couldn't, though. It simply wasn't possible.

Griff seemed to understand her panic attack. Pulling a towel from the rack, he dried himself with a slow precision that eased her nerves. "I didn't expect you to come in here," he said, tucking the towel around his waist and coming to stand just a breath from her.

She gulped, tilting her head back to look at him. Soft, brown eyes twinkled in the stark light of the bathroom, eyes that warmed even as they devoured. "I heard the shower," she said. "I wasn't sure what you wanted me to do."

"You've already done it." He bent his head and touched his lips to hers, withdrawing before she could lean into his kiss. "Why don't you relax and let me do the rest, hmm?"

She instinctively rejected the passive role, wanting more than that would give her. Shaking her head, she unclenched her fingers from her skirt and brought them to his chest, noting with satisfaction the way his breath caught at her touch.

That her fingers weren't quite steady didn't deter her. "I need to be part of this, Griff," she said, tracing the contours of his chest with her fingertips before laying her palms flat against him.

His smile looked a touch forced. "I couldn't do it without you, honey." Resting his forearms on her shoulders, he bent down to nip the curve of her ear.

Lightning shot through her as he soothed the tender shell with his tongue. It was all Sharron could do to submit.

To stand on legs whose muscles had turned to jelly.

And yet it wasn't enough.

He'd shaved that morning, she realized, as she nuzzled her face against his. That was definitely something she needed to talk to him about . . . another time. Her fingers thrust into the hair at the back of his neck, spreading into the thick softness, warming as she was being warmed.

She lifted her mouth and opened it beneath his. Their tongues danced and mated, and she inched forward to stand tightly between his thighs. His hands swept down her back to close over her bottom, pulling her even more closely against him, against the hard evidence of his arousal. He held her firmly, stroking her through her clothing, fitting her to his body without allowing the cloth barriers to fall. Her skirt bunched in his grip, then fell back to her knees, bringing a moan of disappointment to her lips.

He was taking his time. Because she was shy, she knew.

Because her experience was less than his, he didn't want to frighten her.

She needed him to know she wanted him at least as much as he wanted her. More, she mused. Much, much more . . . if that could be possible. A throbbing, wet heat built between her legs, the kind of heat that could know only one kind of relief. She opened her mouth against his chest and tasted his skin, warm and tangy, scented with her soap.

Griff resumed a fevered caress of her back, her buttocks, her thighs. She shimmied against him, the heat of his body sinking into hers, stoking the fire deep within. His mouth found hers again as he set her a slight distance away and quickly worked free the buttons of her blouse. He slipped it from her shoulders, leaving the silk camisole in place as he pushed her skirt from her hips. Softly murmured words of passion and pleasure accompanied his exploration of her body as he slid her lace panties down her thighs to join the pile of clothes on the floor. His mouth followed the downward path of his hands, landing hot, wet kisses on her hip, her thigh, her knee, then all over again, in reverse, as he straightened to stand in front of her, one hand lightly cupping her bottom, the other brushing the long fall of her hair behind her shoulder. Tremors shook her as he hooked a long finger in the delicate strap of her camisole, his gaze hungry yet touched with a patience she wished he'd forget.

Perhaps, Sharron mused, she would have to help him to forget.

A drowsy look came into his eyes as she tugged the towel from his hips and let it fall away. He didn't so much as take a breath in reaction, but his slow smile overflowed with sensual promise.

"You shouldn't have done that, honey," he murmured, his fingers beginning a slow massage across her hip and fanny. "That towel was the only thing keeping me from taking you here and now."

"I thought that was the whole idea," she said, gasping over the words as his fingers danced across the sensitive hollow at the base of her spine. She sank her nails into the tightly corded muscles of his arms, steadying herself in this embrace that kept them inches apart.

"I mean here, in the bathroom," he growled. Both hands at her hips now, he held her back from him, keeping his distance for whatever purpose he had in mind. "The floor, the counter. Either will do, you know, because I really don't think I can walk like this."

"Like what?" But she knew. Her gaze, thus far restricted to his chest and above, fell below his waist. Through half-lowered lids, she saw for the first time the evidence of his desire; saw what she'd felt against the softness of her belly. His arousal was hard, thrusting boldly toward her.

For once in her life, she didn't blush.

She wanted him.

Without being conscious of her intent, Sharron reached down and discovered for herself the exotic wonder of satin over steel.

Griff forced himself to stand still, blood hammering in his ears as her fingers slowly closed around him. His hand clenched her bottom, his fingers digging into the soft muscles in a disordered rhythm that matched the erratic beat of his heart. She held him carefully, then with greater firmness as her shyness completely evaporated, leaving a bold, wanton woman standing before him. His hips bucked as she stroked his hard length, then again as she traced a delicate finger across the blunt, velvety tip. Her smile was filled with wonder, and he groaned aloud as her fingers flexed around him again, with more assurance than before, more confidence.

It was time.

His hand found her wrist, and he tugged with gentle insistence until she let go of his throbbing erection. He pushed her chin up with the back of his knuckles, then slowly put his mouth over hers, watching her gray eyes go almost clear in passion. She made a soft sound of hunger and impatience.

"Hold that thought," he said, then left her standing as he dug through his pile of clothes until his fingers encountered the foil packet of protection he'd brought with him. Ripping it open, he turned and let her watch as he attended to this last, necessary detail. "You've been on the pill less than a month, honey. It's too soon to trust it."

And then she was in his arms, her breasts loose beneath the silk camisole, the hard tips pressing into his chest and driving him over the edge of reason. He took her hips between his hands and lifted, drawing her up his body, urging her with gentle whispers to circle her legs around his waist as he propped himself against the pedestal sink. Her arms snaked around his neck, her mouth pressing hot, frantic kisses on his. Keeping one arm firmly locked around her waist, Griff rubbed her bottom with his other hand, drawing closer and closer to the flowering center of her.

Draped around him as she was, Sharron was completely open to his touch. His knuckles brushed across the swollen flesh once, then again, driving her to bite his shoulder as the ecstasy flowed through her. Tiny cries of pleasure filled the silence around them as he caressed her, his fingers toying with her sensitive nub in between testing her tight sheath.

When he could wait no longer, he eased her down over his throbbing member. Her face came into focus as he entered her, her eyes soft with wonder, her lips parted by a long, luscious moan. Sensual heat flooded through him, and his hips moved reflexively, pushing between the hot petals as he sought to bury himself all the way inside her heat.

Home.

His hands flexed around her hips when she tried to move against him, and he whispered words of praise and need and, yes, of love. Because he loved her, and wanted her to know he didn't take her lightly.

Not now, when he was as close to her as was humanly possible.

Not now, when they were verged on the precipice of a wondrously magical voyage.

She cried out something he didn't understand, but wouldn't say it again when he asked. He didn't push her, thinking this wasn't the time for confessions.

He realized, though, that she hadn't known he loved her, and that puzzled him. He banked that thought for another time.

He felt the sweat break out on his forehead as he luxuriated in the total sense of rightness, of joy. "Let's go to bed," he murmured against her hair as he somehow found the strength to move his legs.

"I thought you said you couldn't walk," she breathed, her teeth sinking into his shoulder.

"Just don't let go, honey. It boggles the imagination what would happen if you fell."

"Depends on how." Her tongue traced the strong line of his neck. "If I went straight down—"

He put an end to her theorizing with a firm pinch on her butt. Mostly, though, he concentrated on getting to the bed. He reached down to throw aside the silk counterpane before easing them both onto cool white sheets, Sharron on her back, urging him down. Her arms pulled his face to meet hers as her legs stayed high above his hips, allowing him deeper access to her warmth, her fire.

He found the yielding luxury of her mouth and fed on it. The kiss began with soft, nibbling touches of his lips on hers, his tongue flicking across her lower lip, then pushing inside for a much needed taste of her sweet mouth. He felt her melt and burn in his arms as he fueled the heat of her mouth with quick, repeated thrusts of his tongue. When he was able to force himself to end the kiss, he braced himself on his elbows and stared deep into wide-open eyes that sparkled and shone with passion in the bright rays of the afternoon sun. She moved restlessly beneath him, and he stilled her with the heavy pressure of his body.

He wanted it to last forever.

Slowly, with a patience he'd never known before, he slipped the chemise up her body until her breasts were bare. The thin fabric stretched tightly above the gentle curves, held in place by his hands as he memorized the beauty he'd revealed. After a long moment, he shifted and allowed her to get free of the camisole, then captured her beneath him once again.

He drew his mouth across the high curve of her breasts, then again, closer this time to the budding tips. He felt the strength of her fingers as they threaded into his hair, guiding him to the sensitive nubs. She let out an almost painful moan when he released a warm breath against her nipples. So sensitive, he remembered, his hips jerking in response to the openness of her need. Whispering soft words of patience and reward, he filled his hands with her flesh and watched with wonder as her growing desire filled her with an exquisite radiance.

Sharron didn't even realize how much her breasts begged to be stroked until he cupped them in his hands and began to prod the hard nipples with his thumbs. When his mouth opened around the crest of one breast, she thought she'd never know a sensation so incredibly delicious.

But that was only the beginning. Griff made love to her with painstaking thoroughness, exploring her, devouring her . . . all without leaving her hot, wet core. He paced them both, teasing and pushing, bringing her back when she would go too far, feel too much. She fought him with laughter and cries of frustration, finding with her hands the parts of him that were sensitive to a light touch, or a more firm one.

They rolled as one across the bed, surging against each other, daring a completion that neither wanted to rush. She knelt over him, his mouth sucking one breast as his hand cupped and teased the other. Her hips moved in a subtle dance, caressing the length of him without completely letting go. Once, twice, then his hands were at her hips, slamming her down against him, rolling her beneath him so that he could set the rhythm.

It was a wild journey as he took her higher than before, further than her imagination had dared soar. Griff sent her skyrocketing over the edge of time itself, then burst into the light beside her, holding her, allowing her to hold him as they fell back to the reality of tangled sheets and sweat-covered bodies.

When they'd caught their breath, they lay facing each other, their hands entwined as they let the afternoon breeze cool their bodies.

He began a different kind of lovemaking then, whispering loving words that held a familiarity and left her wanting more. Love words that translated to praise for her responses, her aggression. Love words that meant something more than sex and less than eternal devotion. She knew that was how it had to be, yet couldn't return them in kind because she couldn't put those kinds of limits on her heart.

That he loved her was a gift she'd not anticipated. He loved her, but their agreement would stand. There wasn't any other choice.

When they were dressed and packed and had gone to Mrs. Claymore's to pick up Harry en route to the airport, Sharron was hard pressed to hide from the two males the fact that she was going to miss the toddler. That she'd miss Griff was beyond needing justification, but Harry . . . Well, that was another matter altogether.

She didn't dare let it show.

Thunk. Thunk. Ker-*thunk*.

Griff stepped out of the shower and paused to listen to the odd noise.

Thunk. Thunk. Boing.

Harry's giggles punctuated the rhythmic noise. Griff snagged a towel from the bar and rubbed it over his hair, wondering what Harry had gotten into now. Only that afternoon, Griff had found Harry shoulder-deep in sweaters that he'd dragged out of Griff's drawers to make a soft landing place for when he jumped off the dresser. That had provoked a double-whammie lecture: Don't jump off the dresser and don't use Daddy's sweaters as a cushion.

Harry had just grinned and asked if that meant he could jump off his top bunk instead. Expanding the no-jump rule to include all high places, Griff wondered if he'd ever get the hang of this parenting routine.

It seemed the only thing keeping him sane were Sharron's nightly calls. She'd been gone five days now, five long, lonely nights during which promises of dreaming of her were all that enticed him into shutting his eyes. She was on his mind constantly, living in his heart now as he grew accustomed to a kind of love unlike that which he lavished on Harry. She didn't believe he loved her, he knew, rationalizing away his words as passionate responses. She'd told him as much, then had said she loved hearing him whisper such nonsense because it made her feel special.

He allowed her to think what she wanted because it was easier that way. Easier than having to tell her that loving made no difference to his stand on marriage.

Easier because he couldn't love her without telling her.

He wondered if she'd ever give those words of love back to him.

Thump. *Ouch!* Boing. Ker-*thunk*.

Griff whipped the towel over his body and pulled on trousers, then went to look for the source of the noise. The thunks, thumps, and giggles amplified as he headed down the stairs. Pausing in the open door to his study, he zeroed in on Harry. His son was sitting cross-legged on the floor, surrounded by assorted office supplies that he'd obviously pulled out of the desk drawer. Harry's fist came down hard on the stapler with a firm ker-*thunk*.

Griff leaned a shoulder against the doorjamb and folded his arms across his chest, his giant sigh causing Harry to look up from his task.

He looked just the slightest bit guilty, but quickly fixed his expression into one of angelic innocence. "Hi, Dad. Nice shower?"

Griff nodded. "Is that a stapler I see there?"

Harry glanced down, then back at Griff, a look of bona fide surprise in his eyes. "Hmm. You're right, Dad. It's a stapler." As in, *how did that get there?*

Griff narrowed his gaze, hoping Harry wouldn't see the muscles twitching at his jaw as he attempted to hold back his grin. "I thought we agreed you weren't to play with the stapler, Harry."

"No, we didn't, Dad. You said you didn't want me stapling your blueprints anymore." He grinned, his expression daring Griff to refute his words.

He couldn't. Griff almost kicked himself for getting that one wrong too. He wondered if he'd learn to say what he meant before Harry went off to college.

Harry swept an arm toward the stack of blueprints. "I didn't staple any of those. You can check."

"I don't need to check, Harry. I trust you." *About as far as I can throw you*, he added under his breath, then put the blame back where it belonged. On himself. He walked over to Harry and hunkered down beside him, glancing over the miscellany his son had processed through the stapler.

His stomach did a half gainer when he saw the little foil packets mixed in with rubber bands, memo sheets, and business cards. Packets from the box of condoms he'd bought last week to protect Sharron from an unwanted pregnancy.

His worst fear was that Harry would ask what they were.

His other worst fear was that he wouldn't be able to think of what to say.

Griff took a deep, calming breath and picked up the stapler. "I don't want you playing with this, Harry. You could put a hole through your finger."

Harry lifted a slightly red digit and stuck it into his mouth. "No kidding. I was lucky I only smashed it a little."

"No more playing with the stapler," Griff reiterated as he pulled Harry's finger from his mouth.

"'kay. I was getting bored anyway."

Griff checked the finger for damage and found nothing worth mentioning. He watched then as Harry picked up a short stack of business cards and began to tug the staple from them.

"What are you doing now, Harry?" He wondered what Harry would do if he sneaked the foil packets out of the pile and hid them in his pocket.

"Takin' out the staples." Harry's brow furrowed as his tiny fingers dug at the bit of metal. "It's hard work, though. Last time, I messed up a couple of your cards when they wouldn't come apart. I had to throw them away."

"Last time?" Griff's stomach began a free-fall that he ignored, as he also disregarded the blood that drained from his face because there was no heartbeat to propel it.

Harry nodded without looking up from his task. "Mm-hmm. I knew you wouldn't want staples in your things, so I took 'em all back out." His elbow shot back as the staple came free from the stack of cards. Harry carefully tossed the metal into the trash and picked up a rubber band. "These are easier, 'cause they bend and pull."

Griff watched with a dry mouth as Harry deftly removed the staple from the rubber band and went on to the next.

"Did you staple all these things before, Harry?"

"Mm-hmm." Harry picked up the foil condom packet and proceeded to tug at the staple. It came free easily, and Harry neatly returned it to its original box. "See how good I put things back, Dad?"

"Mm-hmm."

"Thought there were more before, though," Harry muttered. "I 'member I got all six with one staple." With plodding thoroughness, Harry counted up to five, then searched the area around his knees for more.

He wouldn't find the missing one, Griff realized, sighing weakly as Harry went back to pulling the staples from those he could find.

Griff couldn't even begin to grapple with the implications. His world was in crisis, and all he could think was that he'd need to find a better hiding place for certain things. After all, he took care to keep medicines locked away. And poisonous cleaning products were kept way out of Harry's reach. Sharp knives were in a high cabinet.

Even the toolshed was locked against Harry's curiosity.

It had never occurred to him that Harry would rummage through his desk drawers. After all, he'd never done more than sort through the stuff Griff kept on the desktop. The stapler, tape, et cetera.

Griff gave himself a mental kick in the butt and resolved to bash his head against a cement wall at his first opportunity.

Harry picked up the last foil packet and went to work on it. Griff shut his eyes against the devastating reminder of Harry's ambush, and wondered what Sharron was going to say when he told her.

Not that he had any idea what he'd actually say.

He wouldn't blame her if she never trusted him again.

"Hey, Dad?"

"Yeah, Harry?" Griff opened his eyes. Harry held a packet up between them, and Griff groaned when he noticed several pinpricks of light peeking through.

"What's this?"

TWELVE

Sharron slipped out of the workshop before it was finished, having heard all she wanted about "The Young Performer and Pre-Performance Adrenaline: How to Channel It." Her personal strategy of trying very hard not to throw up before playing to a large crowd wasn't something she'd felt like sharing, although experience had taught her that the unquestionably negative tactic was at least as effective as others she'd heard of over the years.

The hotel buzzed with the late afternoon check-ins as she mounted the stairway leading to the second-floor ballroom. She put her ear to the closed door, listening to ensure all was quiet before peeking inside. The enormous room was empty and dark, the only light coming from a partly open door at the back of the room. Sharron slipped inside and crossed the wide expanse of carpet to the far corner where a grand piano sat in solitary splendor.

Sliding onto the padded bench that was still adjusted for her height, she lifted the keyboard cover and ran her fingers lightly over the keys. The sound was loud in the barren ballroom, even though she'd not bothered to open the lid that covered the strings. Long years of discipline resulted in several minutes of scales and other warm-up exercises before she segued into the first notes of a popular melody. Sharron wasn't really paying attention to what her fingers were doing. Her thoughts were four hundred odd miles to the north, with a man she was coming to know better with each passing day.

Each passing night, rather. Nights that were spent apart yet filled with intimacies she'd shared with no other man. Griff told her secrets in one breath, fantasies in another, then provoked her into returning the favor. Lifelong ambitions were given as much airtime as quirks and habits. Personal histories were shared and dissected, the good parts as well as the bad.

Under his persistent questioning, she told him about her life as a performer, highs and lows alike. The highs were still exhilarating, retold in stunning reviews that she could almost recount from memory.

Then she gave him every excruciating detail of one performance, when she'd become so involved in the music that she'd scooted off the bench and fallen on her tush in front of an audience of thousands.

She listened to Griff's laughter and knew the audience had been kinder in its restraint.

She couldn't hold it against him, though, because by the time she was finished telling him how she'd put her heel through her gown in an attempt to stand, followed by the conductor's efforts to assist her that went awry when she pulled him off balance, Griff had a better picture than had the audience.

He also accused her of making it up.

She let him believe what he wanted.

Sharron smiled, realizing she was playing her favorite ballad from *Les Misérables*. It was a song of dreams and sadness that had succeeded in bringing tears to her eyes more than once . . . yet not today.

No more tears, she'd promised herself.

Today, the ballad found an indulgent audience in her heart, and she turned her thoughts to Harry. What would he think about his father's position on marriage when he was old enough to make those kinds of decisions for himself? Would he be a confirmed bachelor like Griff, or would he pledge his heart to every woman he met?

Would Harry's teenage years be a trial, she wondered, or would he mature to that next level that took the pain out of sixteen and brought confidence to the minds of his girlfriends' parents? She wouldn't know, she realized, just as she'd never watch him ski, skate, or play basketball.

It was hard to anticipate how Harry would develop, even though she felt she knew him quite well. A smile tugged at her heart as she remembered the afternoon naps they'd shared, his tiny frame curled up against her own.

She missed him more than she could afford to let on.

She would exit from their lives the moment it was over between her and his father. And it would be soon, she realized, because she didn't think she could handle being around Griff for long and know that only one thing stood in the way of their shot at a lifetime of happiness together.

One thing, one male: Griff, not Harry. Griff, and his position on marriage. Griff, and his denial that there could ever be a happily-ever-after.

No, Harry wasn't in the way at all. He was too deeply entrenched in her heart to be anything more than a child she loved very, very much. Every morning since her arrival in Los Angeles, Harry called her not long after he'd climbed out of bed, chattering about the past day's activities, the new day yet to unfold . . . and when was she coming back because he missed her?

Her sigh faded as she picked out the notes of a children's song she remembered from years past. Harry was a symptom of a more serious affliction, an excitement so overwhelming, it was all she could do to hide it from Griff.

In the last few days, she'd come to accept that all her previous thoughts on children in general and as they pertained to her life in particular were totally inaccurate. Lack of exposure to children had led her to believe she was not interested in including them in her life. She'd been wrong. More than realizing she loved Harry, Sharron was astonished to discover that it went much deeper, much further than one little boy.

She wanted a child of her own. A baby, a toddler . . . even, God help her, a teenager.

A child as much like Harry as she could manage.

At a loss as to what to play next, she allowed her fingers to caress the keys without striking a single note as she silently reaffirmed her decision to keep this one secret from Griff. In the dark hours of night, though, when she was curled up around the phone, listening to the husky nonsense he badgered her with in between whispers of sensual promise, murmurs of love, she found it almost impossible not to be lulled into believing he would accept her news with joy. And with changes of his own.

Almost impossible, but not quite.

She resisted because there was no other choice.

Griff's telephone rang promptly at nine, just as it had every other night Sharron had been gone. He took the call at his desk, the box of condoms casting a lonely silhouette in the light of a single lamp.

He picked up the phone on the second ring, only taking the time to ensure it was, in fact, Sharron before giving her the grim details.

There was a long silence, then he could have sworn he heard her giggle—which was nonsense because she was probably going to catch the next plan home and take his head off, if not something more pertinent to the disaster.

"Let me get this straight, Griff." Her voice had a strained quality that matched his. "Your son stapled a box of condoms together?"

"And then took out the staples and put them back in the box." Neatly, he reminded himself. So neatly he hadn't noticed.

"So what you're saying is you've got a box of condoms with little holes punched through them?"

He was positive he heard the giggle this time. Stifling a growl of his own, he tried to make it more clear since she was obviously missing the point. "Not a full box, Shar. We used one, remember?"

Sharron remembered. A deep flush warmed her skin, but it was insufficient to ward off the blossoming laughter. The image of Harry industriously stapling a miscellany of items was cute, but when the items in question were condoms, her imagination simply went off the scales.

"Harry admitted he'd done this before," Griff went on. "I figure the chances are about ninety-nine percent that he did it before we made love. Is any of this sinking in yet, honey?"

Griff's stern rebuke stemmed the tide of her laughter . . . for a moment. "Oh, it's sinking in all right," she mumbled, clenching her teeth until her eyes watered. "Tell me, Griff. How do you punish a kid for punching holes in condoms? Take away his Nintendo for a week?" The giggles escaped full force as tears ran down her face.

"This isn't funny!" he roared.

"What's not funny about it? I'd think that anyone who left a box of condoms in the reach of a three-year-old should get everything they've got coming to them." She ignored his shouting with the ease of someone who was not in the least worried about the consequences. Five days without Griff had forced a perspective she found wonderfully comforting.

An unplanned pregnancy held no threat for her, not any longer. She couldn't, naturally, share this little bit of news with him because she was unwilling to take the chance he'd back away, afraid of her intentions.

Which were honorable. She fully intended to honor the terms of their arrangement.

Unless she was pregnant, of course. Then everything would have to change.

Griff's thoughts on marriage, for one. She would have no qualms about showing him how wrong he was if they had indeed created a child between them.

He could blame no one but himself. Or Harry. Sharron burst into a new round of giggles that drowned out whatever Griff was trying to say. When the phone slammed in her ear, she literally howled, holding her sides as she fell back onto the bed.

It rang again five minutes later. She'd almost got herself under control when he set off another gale of laughter by asking, "Do you think you can be sensible about this, Shar?"

No, she didn't think she could. "I'd love to hear what you told Harry when he asked why you turned green."

He muttered something obscene that she was clearly meant to hear. "I turned white, not green," he corrected her. "I swear my heart didn't beat for a full minute."

She felt a touch of sympathy at his predicament. Just a touch, though. "I hope you got your semantics straight with him on this one. What did you say? Something simple like *'Don't staple my condoms together anymore'?*"

"*Dammit*, Sharron! Settle down and quit *joking* about this!" His roar cut across her laughter, and she chose to subdue her response so that he wouldn't take it upon himself to fly to Los Angeles and attempt to fix her attitude problem.

She had no idea how he'd do it, but it wasn't worth taking the chance. Better he should think she wasn't worried, that's all. "Stop your roaring, Griff. You'll wake Harry." As well as most of northern California, she imagined.

The ensuing silence was loud with indignation. "I don't roar, Sharron," he said in a tone that brooked no nonsense. "I'm merely trying to get you to admit the gravity of this mess."

Gravity had nothing to do with it. She grinned, wondering if he'd know she was doing it. "You can calm down, Griff. There's no chance I'm pregnant."

"You mean, you've had your period?" he said in a rush of words that she imagined were filled with relief.

She really couldn't lie. "Not yet, but I really think there's nothing to worry about. I was on the pill," she added with false reassurance.

"Less than a month on the pill isn't a guarantee," he groused. "You heard what the doctor said."

"If I remember, abstinence was all he'd give his support to," she murmured, thankful they hadn't made love before they'd realized she was ill. If she'd become pregnant and gotten chicken pox at the same time . . . The complications boggled the mind. Still, it hadn't happened, and she determinedly searched for more logical reassurances. "I'm sure it was the wrong time of the month, Griff. And besides, even though the . . ." She hesitated, knowing if she said the word condom aloud one more time, she might fall apart all over again. "Even though the product was damaged, I'm convinced it did enough of a job to minimize the risk."

"Minimal risk isn't good enough," he muttered.

"A staple hole is so tiny—"

"Tiny to you or me, but the Holland Tunnel to a sperm."

Trust an architect to put it in structural terms, she mused. "I guess you'll just have to spend the next week or so worrying, won't you?" She knew she wouldn't. "I refuse to make myself crazy over something that's not going to happen."

She decided to buy a pregnancy test kit the minute she got home.

There was a long silence, giving birth to a nervous fluttering in her stomach. When he finally spoke, it was with a sense of acceptance she hadn't heard before. "You're right, honey. I let myself get all worked up over nothing."

And with that, they silently agreed to drop a dangerous subject. They talked for a few minutes longer, confirming her arrival time the next day, Sharron trying to convince him she could take the shuttle bus back north, Griff insisting on coming for her. With Harry, he said, because the toddler had already made his wishes plain on that matter.

They hung up on a note of tenderness that filled her heart with a warmth she was quickly getting used to. He told her he loved her, and she knew that he meant it.

It gave her something to hold on to.

Sharron was grateful he hadn't brought up the subject of her possible pregnancy again. Turning out the light, she rested her arm on her cheek and tried to relax . . . to forget.

It was for the best, she knew. There was nothing to be done about it now. If Griff's worst fears were realized, she could only hope he wouldn't dig his heels in too deeply when she presented the only viable solution: Marriage. After all, he claimed to love her.

The love she felt for him was firmly, permanently ensconced in her heart.

She lay quietly with her hand flat against her stomach, her sense of hope undermined by a niggling worry she couldn't ignore. How early did pregnancy begin to affect a woman? she wondered, remembering the strange lethargy that had been with her most of the day.

How could she sleep without knowing?

Griff tossed the box of condoms into the trash, then looked in on Harry before heading down the hall to his own room. He'd wanted to reassure Sharron, yet she'd ended up reassuring him. Her world might be falling apart, yet she'd defied the calamity with laughter and disavowal that there was any problem at all.

It was for the best, he figured. The "what ifs" would only worry her. If she was pregnant, there was but one thing they could do. He hoped she wouldn't fight him when he dragged her to the altar. Becoming an instant mother to a three-year-old as well as dealing with her first pregnancy were bound to make her a bit testy. But he loved her, and hoped she would learn to love him.

Marriage, he realized, didn't fill him with dread as it had for so many years.

Perhaps it was because he trusted Sharron with his heart . . . with his life.

With his child.

But could he trust himself? Griff lay awake in the darkness and pondered that question until sleep filled his mind with other thoughts, other dreams.

Dreams of Sharron.

Sharron walked off the plane and into the terminal, her gaze drifting over the crowds as she looked for Griff and Harry. The day was suddenly less bright when she realized they hadn't come to the gate to meet her.

No matter. They were probably waiting at the curb. Parking was such a hassle, she told herself as she headed in the direction of the baggage claim area, the lassitude of the previous day still dragging at her steps. The airport was huge, she mused, and by the time a person found a parking place and made his way indoors, thirty minutes were easily consumed. Griff probably hadn't wanted to take the extra time—

A high-pitched giggle was her only warning. In the next second a low-flying bundle of color attached itself to her knees. Sharron fought for balance and was saved by Griff's firm grip on her arm. His other hand slid across her shoulders, and without crushing the boy who was clinging to her legs with the tenacity of a limpet, Griff lowered his head and took her mouth in a hard, fast kiss.

"Welcome home, honey," he murmured, his lips

crooked in a half smile as she eagerly submitted to the two-pronged attack of father and son.

"Hi." Her own greeting was breathless and skimpy, and Griff kissed her again before reaching down to detach Harry. He would have lifted the toddler to ride on his shoulders, but Harry had other ideas, holding out his arms to Sharron in a plea for a hug.

A *long* hug. He stuck his face into the curve of her shoulder, adjusted his bottom to her hip and asked her if she would like it if he hugged her all the way to the car.

She didn't mind, not even when her arms began to ache from holding thirty-odd pounds tight against her chest. Griff, his protest that Sharron couldn't possibly carry Harry all the way to the car being completely ignored, walked beside them, her purse in one hand, his other arm resting lightly on her shoulder.

"You've been gone so long, Shawon. I missed you." Harry's little hands clasped tightly behind her neck, dislodging a few of the pins there that held up her hair.

She couldn't have cared less.

"I missed you too," she murmured, brushing her lips across his soft, curly hair, feeling better than she had in days. "Did your dad tell you I got past level six in the Nintendo game?"

"Mm-hmm. I'm on nine." Harry snuggled closer—if it were possible—and sighed happily against her neck. "Do you like airplanes, Shawon? Dad says we can ride in an airplane when we go to Disneyland."

"You're going to Disneyland? How exciting!" She'd never been.

"Yup! Dad says they have a haunted house and a boat ride through a jungle and all sorts of stuff." He pushed back in her arms to look into her face. "Can you go with us, Shawon? I'll be real good, and you can even have some of my peanuts I'm going to take for the elephants."

"They have elephants?" she asked, unnerved by Harry's unexpected invitation.

"Maybe not there, but Dad says there's a big zoo we can go to. Do you like elephants, Shawon?"

"Well, sure I like—"

"Then you'll come?" he said excitedly.

"Now Harry, I didn't say *when* we were going—" Griff began, but Sharron cut him off so that it wouldn't come down to an argument between father and son.

"I don't see that I'll have time to go, Harry. I've only got a few weeks before I start school, and then my schedule will be filled."

"What about Christmas? Can you go then?"

"Harry, Sharron might want to visit her family at Christmas," Griff said, wishing his son would learn a little tact . . . or patience.

Griff had his own questions to ask her, and her answers would make her presence with them at Disneyland an assumption or a casualty.

He'd get to all that later, during their "adults only" hours.

"But I want her to come with us!" Harry wasn't going to let it go.

Sharron and Griff shared a helpless look before she realized she had the means to divert the toddler. "Did I mention that I brought you something from Los Angeles?"

Harry perked up immediately. "You did?"

"Yup. It's in my suitcase." She hitched Harry more securely over her hip and tweaked his nose. "Maybe if you're real good, I'll let you open it when we get to the car."

"I can be real good, Shawon. Can't I, Dad?"

Griff mumbled something that ended with "every other leap year" and pulled Sharron closer to his side as the crowds thickened near the entrance to the concourse. When they finally arrived at the luggage turntables, Griff led them to a quiet corner before joining the throng awaiting their bags.

Sharron put Harry on his feet and dug into her purse for a tissue and used it to wipe the perspiration from the back of her neck. Carrying Harry was wearing her down faster than she would have thought possible, she mused as she fanned her face with her hand. Then again, it was probably just too warm in the terminal.

She felt much as she had the day she'd been diagnosed with chicken pox.

Leaning against a cool wall, she continued to fan herself and keep an eye on Harry, who had pushed through the crowd to join his father. Griff shot a look over his shoulder to make sure she was where he'd left her, then leaned down to keep Harry from catching his fingers in the conveyor belt. The two blond heads disappeared from sight as more people crowded around.

Disneyland. She envied Harry his trip.

Sharron had wanted to go there as a child, but there had never been enough time. Between her practice schedule and her parents' commitments, she'd managed to grow up without shaking hands with Mickey Mouse. And now, as much as the child in her wanted to say yes to Harry's wild invitation, she knew better than to imagine Griff would agree.

It would be too much of a family thing for them to travel together, to Disneyland or anywhere else.

No, Griff wouldn't go for that.

Besides, she had other things to do with her time. Lots of things.

Things she couldn't for the life of her remember.

Harry talked to his new stuffed dinosaur all the way back through San Francisco and across the Golden Gate Bridge as Griff and Sharron rehashed the week's events, things they'd already discussed over the phone but which, somehow, needed repeating. In no time at all, it seemed, they were pulling up in front of her home. Both Griff and Harry helped carry her things inside, then Griff sent Harry outside to play so he could give Sharron a proper welcome-home kiss.

His mouth was gentle on hers, undemanding because he knew better than to let it get too hot. But he hadn't reckoned on Sharron, a woman who continued to surprise him with every breath she drew. Her response was gentle, too, until she slid her arms around his neck and pressed her body hard against his. Everything changed then, and the control he'd exerted shattered and fell apart around them. The kiss became hard, hot, and consuming, taking him back to the day they'd made love on the bed just a few feet away.

It was all he could do not to drag her down the hall and do it again, make love to her until neither of them had the energy to stand or even breathe.

"Can we rent a Nintendo game this afternoon, Dad? There's a new one I want to show Shawon." Harry pushed open the café doors from the living room and looked expectantly at the adults, who had only just managed to break the passionate kiss a heartbeat before. Griff carefully pulled Sharron's arms from his shoulders, kissed her on the forehead, and murmured something about later.

Clearing his throat, he then turned to his son. "May I rent a game, Harry. May I, not can I."

Harry grinned. "Does that mean yes?"

Griff just shook his head and said, "We'll see. I need to get to a meeting, and I don't know if I'll have enough time to swing by the rental place on the way to Mrs. Claymore's."

"I'll take him," Sharron said. She hid her disappointment that Griff had to work, then realized that perhaps it was for the best because she had an errand of her own to run that she wasn't willing to share with him.

Not yet.

"You don't mind?" Griff checked his watch and winced. "I really do need to get going."

She shook her head. "You go on ahead. Harry and I will run over to the store, then I'll take him by Mrs.

Claymore's." After they stopped at the pharmacy, she added silently.

She couldn't stand not knowing.

She hadn't counted on the curiosity of a three-year-old. Sharron found an entire shelf filled with a variety of pregnancy-testing kits and knew she'd underestimated the task at hand. Not only would she have to read each and every one to find which was appropriate for her situation, she had to do it with Harry dogging her heels. Trying to act nonchalant, she picked one out and started to read the back of the package.

"What's that, Shawon?"

She slid him a patient glance. "Just something I need to buy, Harry. Why don't you look at the directions to your Nintendo game?"

"I can't read." He edged closer to her legs. "It's cold in here, Shawon."

She scooped him up in one arm and held the package in her other hand, trying to see if this was one she could use at anytime during the day. It wasn't, and she put it back, selecting another.

"Why does that have a picture of a pregnant mommy on it?" Harry reached out to touch the package.

Sharron put that one back, too, exchanging it for one without a picture. "I don't know, Harry. Are you sure you can't read?"

He nodded vigorously. "I know my letters, though." He squinted at the package. "P-r-e-g-n—"

"You're getting too heavy, kiddo," she interrupted, putting him back on his feet.

"Can we go yet, Shawon?"

"You bet." Gritting her teeth, Sharron picked out two packages at random and caught Harry's hand. "Mrs. Claymore is probably wondering where you are."

"I'll carry those for you."

It was a miracle she made it out of the store with even a shred of her dignity still intact.

Griff's meeting got out early, and he took advantage of the lull in his schedule to run by the florist and pick up the flowers he'd ordered that morning. They were arranged in a vase he and Harry had found earlier that week. It had taken nearly a full day's shopping before Harry had decided on a vase he thought Sharron would like. Replacing the one he'd broken had become an obsession for the child, and while he had to rely on his father to shoulder the financial responsibility, he was determined she would know how sorry he'd been to break the other.

Harry's actual words had been somewhat simpler. "It's important Shawon know I'm not bad."

Griff didn't think that was an issue. He agreed to pay for the vase out of Harry's nonexistent allowance—about three years' worth, he figured.

The flowers were Griff's idea.

Propping the huge arrangement on the floor of the backseat, Griff drove home and called Mrs. Claymore to say he'd be a little early picking up Harry. That way, they could take the vase by Sharron's together before the flowers wilted in the car. He figured he had an hour before he had to leave, an entire hour in which he didn't have a meeting or plans that had to be drawn or a small boy demanding his attention.

An hour to figure out how he was going to propose to Sharron. Propose marriage. The big "M."

Happily ever after.

He poured himself a glass of iced tea and took it out onto the patio. Settling into a cushioned chair, Griff put his feet up on another chair and wished he'd proposed before he told her about the stapler incident.

But then, he hadn't realized he wanted to spend the rest of his life with her until after they'd had that conversation. It was her reaction that had got him thinking, her laughter.

Her gentle teasing about something that might change her entire life. He'd known then that he wanted to spend his life loving her.

He'd told her before that he loved her. He thought she might believe him, but with reservations because that's the way they'd set things up. Reservations that gave the words a conditional meaning.

There were no longer any conditions.

He intended to ask her tonight, before she knew if she was pregnant or not. She was going to argue with him, he realized, because he'd been so adamant about the subject of marriage.

So damned bullheaded!

Griff remembered the words he'd said to her the night

he'd proposed their arrangement. *I won't marry again, Sharron. Not ever. It wouldn't be fair to get involved with you without making that clear.*

He hadn't known then how deeply in love he'd fall with her.

He hadn't realized that the threat of life without her filled him with a sense of emptiness he couldn't bear.

Harry loved her too. Griff smiled as he stared blankly across the green lawn, wondering if he'd known back then how big an influence Harry would have in this decision. Had Griff decided to show Sharron her maternal instincts were fully functioning because he knew it would be important to their future?

Or had he fallen in love with the woman who loved his son?

He wished he had known before. If she was pregnant, she might think he was marrying her out of duty.

He wasn't. He intended to marry her whether or not they'd created a baby that one perfect time they'd made love.

But how could he get that across to her without leaving doubts in her mind? Doubts that might make her say no.

He could only hope she wasn't pregnant. Then she would have to believe him.

THIRTEEN

She was pregnant.

Sharron stared at the results for a full minute before ripping open the second package and doing it all over again. Ten minutes later, she had her confirmation.

Unless both tests were wrong, she was definitely pregnant. Maybe. She reread the instructions—all of them this time—and discovered the accuracy was dependent upon the tests being taken three days after a missed period. She couldn't wait that long.

Sharron walked into the bedroom and dialed the number of her doctor. Perhaps he could do it faster, she thought as she waited for the secretary to pick up the line.

She couldn't stand being the only one who knew, and she did know she was pregnant.

She had to tell Griff.

The secretary answered before Sharron figured out how she was going to do that. No, the doctor wasn't in for the rest of the week, and neither was his nurse. Would she care to wait until the following Monday?

No, she wouldn't. Sharron explained her situation and was referred to a Planned Parenthood clinic. They could do the test there and have the answer the same day. And, yes, the blood test would definitely confirm pregnancy three days after conception.

She called and made an appointment for the following morning.

She decided to wait until then to tell Griff, because it was no use getting him involved if the first results had been wrong.

Singing a nursery rhyme under her breath, Sharron walked over to her closet and reached for the scarlet silk dress. It was time to fulfill his fantasy.

And hers.

She carefully lay the dress on the bed and sorted through her lingerie drawer for the bits and pieces that she would wear underneath it. It didn't take long, because the strapless dress didn't need more than a slip, stockings, and something to hold them up. She held out a pair of lacy panties and debated whether she even needed them, then burst into laughter and threw them onto the bed with the rest.

Then she went into the living room to practice because Griff wasn't due for hours yet and she couldn't very well stand around giggling all afternoon.

It never occurred to her to worry about what he would say when she brought up the subject of marriage.

The man she loved would do the right thing.

Griff heard the music as he came up the walk. He paused at the front door, recognized the rambunctious Rachmaninoff melody, and realized Sharron's gay, giggly mood hadn't subsided much from that afternoon when he and Harry had brought over the flowers. She'd been playing the piano then, too, the first time she'd done so in his presence.

She was better than good. She was marvelous on the instrument. And incredibly energetic.

He wondered if she was always so aggressive in her approach to music. The energy with which she attacked the keys made him realize she hadn't been joking when she'd related the story about falling off the bench.

He'd be surprised if it had only happened once.

Taking care not to make any noise—not that Sharron would notice, as involved as she was in the music—Griff let himself into the house. He walked into the living room until he could see the end of the piano. The flowers were where she'd put them, on the closed lid of the piano. He marveled that the music could still be so loud when the lid was closed, and decided the neighbors were lucky he'd brought the flowers, because she'd really blast them out if the lid were raised.

The flowers and vase had been a huge hit. She'd swept Harry into a giant hug, then kissed Griff with a passion that was totally bereft of any shyness whatsoever. Harry had beamed at the hug, stayed miraculously silent during the kiss, then pulled Griff back out the door because he still hadn't played the rented Nintendo game and it was due back the following day.

Griff edged farther around the corner and was confronted by a surprise he hadn't anticipated.

She was wearing the dress, a wonder of scarlet silk that clung to her breasts and underscored the perfection of her creamy skin. Her hair was swept up and off her shoulders in a fancy knot that looked as though it depended on a single pin for stability.

His fantasy. A bolt of pure, male satisfaction shot through him, and he held himself perfectly still as the woman of his dreams filled his heart with music and love.

He couldn't imagine a life without her.

The music ended in a splendid crash of sound that pulsed through him in a rhythm that gradually became more shallow as he adjusted to the sudden silence. Sharron looked up then, and he saw something special in her eyes that he'd never seen before.

He saw a love and happiness that mirrored what was in his own heart. One minute it was there . . . and then it was gone, a trick of the light, perhaps. Or was she thinking she needed to hide it from him?

He'd set her straight about that before the night was over.

She rose from the piano bench and walked very slowly around the piano, her fingers dancing across the polished ebony wood, her expression hidden behind lowered lashes. Griff watched with his heart thudding against his chest, thinking how incredibly beautiful she was . . . and how much he wanted to see again that look of love in her eyes.

Sharron had known the moment Griff entered the house, so attuned was she to his presence. In that moment, she'd realized there was no way she could persuade him to marry her if he wasn't convinced that she loved him. One thing at a time, she'd told herself as her fingers had raced through the final bars.

Tonight, she would tell him she loved him. Tonight, in the comfort of his arms when saying such things was natural and, yes, a great deal easier than, for example, blurting it out over the dinner table.

Tomorrow, she would tell him the rest. After her appointment, when there was absolutely no doubt about the life they'd created.

She stopped beside the flowers and lifted her lashes to look at the man who had stolen her heart. He didn't look like a bandit, she mused, a smile curving her lips as her eyes feasted on the handsome, all-male figure who stood just a few feet away. Dressed rather impressively in a boldly colored tie and dark jacket over wheat-colored slacks and shirt, he held his ground. Waiting for her, she realized.

Then, suddenly, she knew what he was waiting for.

"I love you." The words left her lips before she'd realized she was going to say them, spoken with more ease than she'd envisioned.

His hands fisted at his sides, and he shook his head in awe. "I didn't expect that, not yet."

"I've loved you for what seems an eternity," she murmured. "I tried not to, but my heart kept getting in the way of my determination."

"Why?"

"The agreement. I knew that falling in love with you would make it harder to keep to the terms." Her fingers flexed around the piano top, the heavy weight of anxiety settling uneasily in her stomach. If he told her now that the terms would never change, she knew her pregnancy would have to remain her secret.

She wouldn't force a man to marry her, not even one who claimed to love her.

His eyes blazed with the passion of love. "Damn the agreement. I wasn't thinking straight then. I am now."

"You are?"

His smile was gentle. "Will you marry me, Shar? Live with me, be my wife?"

She felt fear then as she never had before. Did he know she was pregnant? Could he be changing the rules for that reason . . . and that reason only?

She had to know. "Why?"

He looked confused. "Because I love you."

It wasn't enough. "You've said that before. Why now, Griff? Why ask me to marry you now?"

She looked so worried and scared that it was all Griff could do not to take her into his arms, bring her the peace and joy he felt deep in his soul because of her. Instead, he kept his distance, willing her to listen with her heart. "I fell a little in love with you the very first time I saw you. Do you remember, Shar? How outraged you were when you thought I was neglecting Harry?

Her nod was barely discernible, and he continued without pausing because it was important she know he was telling the truth. "I fell in love with you, then kept falling until I woke up to the fact that my life wasn't threatened by that love. I trust you with my heart, Sharron," he said softly. "Will you trust me with yours for the next few decades or more?"

"You said love was a silly basis for marriage," she reminded him. "That a man in love couldn't trust his instincts. The agreement—"

He waved her quiet with his hand. "The agreement was the act of a desperate man who was afraid of what he was beginning to feel for you." He gave a short, self-deprecating laugh, then captured her gaze with his. "I was wrong, Sharron. Just like you were wrong."

Her smile was a brave rebuttal. "I'm never wrong."

"What about Harry? Tell me you don't want to be his mother." His voice lowered, and there was a tenderness in every word as he said, "Tell me you don't want to give birth to our child."

She couldn't, and he could see that in her expression before she said a single word. "Harry is easy to love," she murmured, then asked the sixty-four-thousand-dollar question. "Will you marry me tonight, Griff? Fly with me to Reno and take me for your wife . . . before we know if I'm pregnant?"

He grinned. "I've always thought red was a great color for a wedding dress."

She gulped. "And if I'm not pregnant?"

"We've got a lifetime to work on that. Beginning tonight." He held out a hand that shook with the emotions that roiled through him. "Let's go get Harry, love.

He'll never forgive us if we take a plane ride without him."

It was going to be okay, Sharron thought. Very okay. She took a deep cleansing breath, then walked toward him with a provocative swing of her hips. "Is this what you had in mind, Griff?" she asked, her fingers brushing across her bare shoulders, then swirling the short, full skirt. "Are you sure you want to spend the night in an airplane when we could be adding new scenes to your fantasy?"

She placed her hand in his and was drawn into his warm embrace. He held her carefully, brushing light kisses on her shoulders, her face, her arms. "I want to spend the night with you, the *whole* night," he murmured into her hair. "If getting married is the only way I can do that, then let's get going."

Sharron wrapped her arms around his waist and wondered why she'd ever imagined she'd need to be the one doing the convincing.

Griff lifted her chin with his knuckles. "What do you say, Shar? Will you marry me tonight?"

Somehow, she knew it was the right thing to do. So Sharron said yes, then grinned because his wedding gift was going to knock him off his feet.

More excited than a couple of teenagers, they flew off to Reno and were married before midnight.

Harry gave away the bride, but was calling her mommy long before they even landed in Reno.

She wore Griff's fantasy dress, then forgot about nonsense things like clothes and convention as Griff slid his grandmother's ring on her finger and pledged to love her forever.

They flew straight back home because Griff had a meeting with the city council the next morning and couldn't afford to miss it. Remembering her own appointment, Sharron didn't mind, though she did point out he wasn't going to be at his best after an entire night without sleep.

He just grinned, and said he'd certainly try to give her his best after they put Harry to bed.

But there were no jokes between them as they walked hand in hand toward Griff's bedroom, no teasing as they undressed each other and slid beneath the sheets.

There was only love.

Griff rose early and dressed for his meeting, then kissed Sharron good morning and good-bye as she lay exhausted amidst the tangled sheets. "I'll call Mrs. Claymore and ask her to pick up Harry in an hour so you can get some rest today. Sure you don't mind giving him breakfast?"

She threw a pillow at him and told him to quit treating her like a guest. "I'm Harry's mom. I'm supposed to do things like that."

"Then the next time he throws up, I'll let you take care of it."

She threw another pillow and said they'd negotiate. "Why don't I drop Harry by Mrs. Claymore's? I've got some errands I need to do this morning."

Griff agreed, then pulled a T-shirt from a drawer and

handed it to her. "In case Harry comes barging in," he said. He gave her a last long, hard kiss and was out the door before she caught her breath. Moments later, she heard Harry stirring down the hall. She'd just managed to pull the T-shirt over her hips when a bundle of energy zipped in the door and made a direct hit on her stomach.

Harry failed to notice his new mommy was a tad winded as he snuggled close against her. "What are we going to do today, Mommy? Can we play in the garden?"

She simply didn't have the heart to tell him he was supposed to go to Mrs. Claymore's. Wrapping her arms around the small, warm body, she thought about her appointment and decided it wouldn't be a problem if she took him along. She'd cancel if she had to.

Today was her first day with her new son.

So Sharron and Harry made plans and separated only as long as it took to get dressed. Sharron showered, then pulled on a white sundress. She was grateful Griff had thought to tell her to pack a few things, because the scarlet dress was definitely inappropriate for the morning's activities. Harry picked out green shorts, a yellow top, and blue shoes.

She wondered how long that stage was going to last because her eyes hurt from looking at him.

While Harry breakfasted on frozen waffles and orange juice, Sharron called the clinic and discovered there was a day-care right next door where she could leave Harry for the few minutes it would take for her test. When she explained to Harry that she had a quick doctor's appointment, he said he wouldn't mind waiting at the day-care.

As long as she hurried. They had lots of things to do.

He wanted to buy film for the camera so they could take pictures of their new family. And bake cookies. And go to the park. And go on a picnic.

Sharron called Mrs. Claymore to tell her Harry wouldn't be coming after all, then buckled Harry into his car seat which Griff had thoughtfully transferred to her car.

She wondered if she was truly pregnant.

She wondered if Harry would mind.

She wondered if she should have told Griff after all.

Wagner was a small town, and as happens frequently in small towns, very little goes on that doesn't get noticed. It wasn't so unusual, then, that Griff happened to be coming out of the courthouse at the same time Sharron was walking toward a building on the opposite corner. He waved his arm and yelled, but traffic in the street between them must have masked his shouts, because she skipped up the stairs and disappeared inside the building without turning around.

He was halfway across the street before he remembered the Planned Parenthood clinic was the only thing inside that building.

Planned Parenthood. Why was Sharron going there? he wondered, waiting for a car to pass before jogging the rest of the way to the curb. His briefcase in one hand, Griff slowed to a walk as he headed toward the clinic. Brent Lawrence had his office several blocks away in a medical building that housed several other doctors and a pharmacy. He knew that because he'd had to go by there to pick up Sharron's calamine lotion.

Planned Parenthood clinics were equipped to offer a variety of services, he knew, yet he could only think of one that Lawrence might not provide.

Abortion.

He came to an abrupt stop as the reality of it hit him between the eyes. Sharron had never said she wanted to have his child. She'd never actually said the words.

He'd married her because he loved her.

She'd married him because she loved him . . . but apparently she didn't trust him enough to share this decision.

A man doesn't have any control over who he falls in love with. History is filled with idiots who loved the wrong woman. My judgment was impaired once. There's nothing to say it wouldn't happen again.

History was repeating itself. The acrid taste of bile filled his mouth.

How could he have been so wrong about her?

Griff's heart pounded in his chest as he stood on the sidewalk and waited for her to come out.

"Hey, Dad!"

Griff could have sworn he heard his son's voice. He turned his head and discovered the multicolored kid clinging to the other side of a chain-link fence. His gaze swept over the playground behind the fence, and he realized it must be some sort of day-care facility.

He couldn't believe Sharron had brought Harry there,

to wait as she did whatever she was doing next door. Abortion counseling, abortion, whatever.

Just one of those errands she'd mentioned.

He forced a smile for his son as he walked over to him, but the effort cost him so much he quit trying. "What are you doing here, Sport?"

"Mommy had a 'pointment. I can't go in with her."

No kidding. Griff hunkered down to his son's level and wished the previous night had never happened. Getting Shawon out of Harry's life would have been enough of a mess.

Getting Mommy out was going to break Harry's heart.

"Want to go to lunch with Dad?" he asked, thinking only that he needed to get Harry away from there before Sharron came out again.

A woman came up behind Harry and put her hand on his shoulder. "Harry, do you know this man?"

Harry giggled. "It's my dad. He's going to take me to lunch."

The woman gave Griff an unsmiling look. "I'm sorry, sir, but the rules don't allow for that. Harry's mother didn't put anyone else's name down for pickup when she signed him in. I can't let you take him."

"But he's my son."

"He's my dad." Harry squirmed out from under the woman's hand and lifted his arms to his father. "I want to go."

"You can't, Harry," the woman said. "You have to wait for your mommy."

"You can't keep him from me," Griff insisted, dropping his briefcase as his gaze measured the height of the fence. "If I have to come over there and take him from you, I will."

Alarm clear on her face, the woman grabbed Harry and was backing off when another voice joined the melee.

"It's all right, Mrs. Kostler. Harry can go with his dad if he wants."

Griff kept his gaze focused on the woman holding Harry, not daring to look at Sharron because she'd see the disappointment in his eyes and he wasn't ready to talk about it.

He didn't know if he ever could.

Mrs. Kostler let Harry go, and he ran back to the fence. "It's too tall, Dad. You'll have to come around."

Sharron touched Griff on the arm. "I'll get him, Griff. I have to sign him out anyway. Why don't you meet us at the car?" She pointed to where her car was parked just down the street. "I'm sorry, Mrs. Kostler. I had no idea my husband would be dropping by. Next time, I'll remember to put his name on the list."

Mrs. Kostler mumbled something about rules, then followed Harry as he sped into the building to wait for Sharron.

Sharron had known something was wrong from the moment she'd heard the rough, strained quality in Griff's voice when he'd threatened to climb the fence. It was more than anger because someone was keeping him from his son.

She knew from the way he refused to look at her that something was very wrong indeed.

She had to know what it was. "What is it, Griff? What's so awful that you can't even look at me?"

He turned to her then, his gaze going beyond her shoulder to the building at her back, the Planned Parenthood clinic. She was confused only as long as it took her to remember the other services offered there and to connect them with Griff's personal history.

Was their marriage over before it had begun? she wondered. Her mouth was dry, and her hands trembled at her sides as she held his condemning stare. "I love you, Griff. All I can say about what you're obviously thinking is if you can't trust yourself, then you'll never trust me."

His brow furrowed, and his words were a rough growl. "What do you mean, trust myself? That isn't what this is about."

She clenched her teeth in frustration because he was being such a damned idiot and couldn't see it. "When your first marriage ended in divorce, you said you'd never marry again because you couldn't trust your instincts. Last night, you told me you'd been wrong . . . and I was foolish enough to believe you."

His face darkened in anger. "You were in that clinic—"

"Yes, Griff, I was in that clinic." Her eyes filled with tears, but she refused to let them get in the way of what needed to be said. "I was in that clinic, and all you have to do is ask and I'll tell you what I was doing there. Right now, though, I'm going inside the day-care to pick up Harry. I'll bring him to you, and then maybe you can explain to him why his new mommy isn't coming home with him."

She turned away to walk toward the entrance, but Griff's hand on her arm held her still. When she looked at him over her shoulder, she saw confusion written all over his expression. "What's the matter, Griff? Worried that your son might not understand?" She shook her head in despair. "Just tell him Shawon's not mommy material after all."

She jerked her arm from his grasp and fled inside, wondering if everyone's first day of marriage went this badly. Then she remembered she'd given the clinic Griff's number to call when the test results were known. Forcing a smile for Harry and creating an excuse to explain why he needed to ride in his father's car, she walked him outside to where Griff was waiting beside her car. Without looking at Griff, she pulled out Harry's car seat and put it down on the sidewalk.

Then she headed back down the street to the clinic, where she crossed Griff's phone number off the form and filled in her own. The Lord only knew how long it would take Griff to come to his senses.

FOURTEEN

Griff was pretty sure Sharron didn't know he was following her.

He was afraid that if he waited until she got home and locked the door behind her, she'd resist opening it again. Then he'd have to break a window or something, and that wouldn't make any points in his favor. He'd do whatever it took, though, because there were a few things that needed to be said before she walked out of his life forever.

He figured that by staying close on her tail, she'd have to let him inside or risk causing a scene on her own front lawn.

Either way, he intended to settle this before another hour passed.

He'd watched her go back into the Planned Parenthood clinic and had been struck by a truth that had eluded him before. Sharron wouldn't do the unthinkable behind his back. She wouldn't do it at all.

His instincts screamed the truth in one ear even as

Harry screamed in his other, wailing something about wanting Mommy and why wasn't she coming with them?

Griff trusted his instincts, trusted Sharron. He prayed she could find it in herself to forgive him when he told her what an ass he'd been.

He couldn't think of a single reason that she should . . . except that she loved him. Or had he destroyed that too?

He'd calmed Harry with soothing promises, then dropped him by Mrs. Claymore's with the explanation that, "Daddy needs to spend some private time with Mommy."

Harry had understood, although he'd pointed out that he went to bed awfully early and when was he going to get to play with his new mommy?

Later, Griff had told him, then sped off toward Sharron's house. It had been luck that he'd caught up with her just a few blocks from her house, and now his hands were gripping the wheel with a force that made his knuckles ache.

She pulled into her drive and he followed her, blocking her exit in case she decided to leave before he'd had his say. Slowly, Griff climbed out of the car and went to meet her as she slipped from hers.

He expected tears, but Sharron welcomed him with a warm, loving smile that almost knocked him off his feet. It drove whatever he was going to say right out of his mind. She leaned back against the side of her car and held his confused gaze with a mischievous one of her own.

"Why are you smiling?" he asked quietly, moving nearer as he realized that was what she wanted. She lifted her arms and slid them around his neck, bringing his head down close to hers.

"I'm smiling, Griff, because it took you less than twenty minutes to realize what a jerk you were being. I'd figured it would take at least an hour." She kissed his chin and asked him if he would put his arms around her waist and hold her tight. Unless he was worried about what the neighbors might think.

The neighbors were the least of his worries. Griff slipped his arms around her, taking care as he brought her hard against him, scarcely believing she wanted to be held by this jerk she'd married less than twenty-four hours before. "I was wrong," he said, rubbing his chin across the top of her head. "Wrong and stupid. You'd never do anything that important without discussing it with me."

"I'd never do it at all," she whispered. "But you knew that all along. You just weren't listening to yourself."

"But what if—"

She covered his lips with the fingers of one hand, looking at him with a stern expression. "I wouldn't have fallen in love with a man who didn't trust himself. It was all a matter of getting you to realize it."

"It was a hard lesson, honey. You turned my world on end."

She shook her head, her eyes brightening to a silver glaze. "*You* turned your world on end. I merely waited for you to put it back to rights." She rested her cheek against his thudding heart. "I'm just glad it didn't take too long for you to realize what an ass you were being."

His mouth wandered across her forehead and past her

fluttering lashes. "Since when did you get so damned smart?"

"I'm not sure that marrying an ass is considered smart—"

He bent and put his mouth over hers before she could finish, which was just as well because she really didn't want to talk.

She wanted to love this man who was her husband.

Griff must have felt the same, because he swept her into his arms and carried her inside . . . where he showed her in private just how much he loved her.

There were no doubts left between them.

It wasn't all that long before they went to Mrs. Claymore's to pick up Harry, but so much had changed since they'd last seen him.

He'd grown, Sharron insisted, tickling him behind the knees to his shrill cries of glee.

"I didn't grow, Mommy. People don't grow that fast."

"Well, Harry, you must have grown, because this morning you were a little boy, and now I know you're going to be a big brother. How can that happen if you haven't grown?"

"I'm going to have a brother?" His eyes were round with excitement.

"Or a sister. We'll have to wait awhile before any of us knows the answer to that." Sharron slid a quick look at Harry's father, who was still looking shell-shocked. She swallowed back tears of happiness, then mouthed a silent "thank you" to him for the privilege of sharing their news with Harry. The toddler gave a war whoop of happiness, threw his arms around her neck, and tumbled them both to the ground.

She gathered he was in favor of the plan.

Griff watched the two rolling on the grass and knew that the sloppy kisses Harry was bestowing on Sharron were a memory she'd carry in her heart the rest of her life, the gift of a child who was now as much her son as he was Griff's.

And then, because raising Harry had taught him that dreams were for living, Griff crawled over to the two people he loved more than anything in the world and launched a surprise tickle attack.

Sharron howled, Harry screamed, and the neighborhood reverberated with the sounds of a family at play.

A noisy family, but one that knew the value of love.

THE EDITOR'S CORNER

It's summertime, and nothing makes the living as easy—and exciting—as knowing that next month six terrific LOVESWEPTs are coming your way. Whether you decide to take them to the beach or your backyard hammock, these novels, written by your favorite authors, are guaranteed to give you hours of sheer pleasure.

Lynne Bryant leads the line-up with **BELIEVING HEART,** LOVESWEPT #630—and one tall, dark, and dangerously handsome hero. Duke King is head of his family's oil company, a man nobody dares to cross, so the last thing he expects is to be shanghaied by a woman! Though Marnie MacBride knows it's reckless to rescue this mogul from a kidnapping attempt single-handedly, she has no choice but to save him. When she sails off with him in her boat, she fancies herself his protector; little does she know that under the magic of a moonlit sky, serious, responsible Duke will throw caution to the wind and, like a swashbuckling pirate, lay claim to the potent pleasures of her lips. Marnie makes Duke think of a seductive sea witch, a feisty Venus, and he's captivated by the sweet magic of her spirit. He wishes he could give her a happy ending to their adventure together, but he knows he can never be what she wants most. And Marnie finds she has to risk all to heal his secret pain, to teach his heart to believe in dreams once more. Lynne has written a beautiful, shimmering love story.

With **ALL FOR QUINN**, LOVESWEPT #631, Kay Hooper ends her *Men of Mysteries Past* series on an unforgettable note—and a truly memorable hero. You've seen Quinn in action in the previous three books of the series, and if you're like any red-blooded woman, you've already lost your heart to this green-eyed prince of thieves. Morgan West certainly has, and that lands her in a bit of a pickle, since Quinn's expected to rob the Mysteries Past exhibit of priceless jewelry at the museum she runs. But how could she help falling under his sensual spell? Quinn's an international outlaw with charm, wit, and intelligence who, in the nine and a half weeks since they have met, has stolen a necklace right off her neck, given her the mocking gift of a concubine ring, then turned up on her doorstep wounded and vulnerable, trusting her with his life. Even as she's being enticed beyond reason, Quinn is chancing a perilous plan that can cost him her love. Pick up a copy and treat yourself to Kay at her absolute best!

Ruth Owen made quite a splash when Einstein, the jive-talking, TV-shopping computer from her first LOVESWEPT, **MELTDOWN,** won a special WISH (Women in Search of a Hero) award from *Romantic Times.* Well, in **SMOOTH OPERATOR,** LOVESWEPT #632, Einstein is back, and this time he has a sister computer with a problem. PINK loves to gamble, you see, and this keeps Katrina Sheffield on her toes. She's in charge of these two super-intelligent machines, and as much as the independent beauty hates to admit it, she needs help containing PINK's vice. Only one person is good enough to involve in this situation—Jack Fagen, the security whiz they call the Terminator. He's a ruthless troubleshooter, the kind of man every mother warns her daughter about, and though Kat should know better, she can't deny that his heat brands her with wildfire. When it becomes obvious that someone is trying to destroy all she's worked for, she has no choice but to rely on Jack to prove her innocence. Superbly combining humor and sensuality, Ruth delivers a must-read.

STORMY WEATHER, LOVESWEPT #633, by Gail Douglas, is an apt description for the turbulent state Mitch Canfield finds himself in from the moment Tiffany Greer enters his life. Though she isn't wearing a sarong and lei when he first catches sight of her, he knows instantly who the pretty woman is. The native Hawaiian has come to Winnipeg in the winter to check out his family's farm for her company, but she's got all the wrong clothes and no idea how cold it can be. Though he doubts she'll last long in the chilly north, he can't help feeling possessive or imagining what it would be like to cuddle with her beside a raging fire—and ignite a few of his own. It seems he's spending half his time making serious promises to himself to keep his hands off her, and the other half breaking those promises. Tiffany wants to keep her mind on business, but she's soon distracted by the cool beauty of the land around her and exhilarated by Mitch's potent kisses. Then she runs into the impenetrable barrier of his mysterious hurt, and she knows she's facing the biggest challenge of her life—to convince Mitch that his arms are the only place she'll ever feel warm again. Gail's luminous writing is simply irresistible.

If intensity is what you've come to expect from a novel by Laura Taylor, then **HEARTBREAKER,** LOVESWEPT #634, will undoubtedly satisfy you. After an explosion renders Naval Intelligence officer Micah Holbrook sightless, he turns furious, hostile, desperate to seize control of his life—and also more magnificently handsome than ever, Bliss Rowland decides. Ever since he saved her life years ago, she's compared every other man she's ever met to him, and no one has measured up. Now that he's come to the island of St. Thomas to begin his recuperation under her care, the last thing she intends to allow is for him to surrender to his fear. It's hard fighting for a man who doesn't want to fight to get better, and the storm of emotions that engulfs them both threatens to destroy her soul. Unsure of his recovery, Micah keeps pushing her away, determined to ignore his hunger to caress her silken skin and the taste of longing on her lips. Knowing that only her passion can heal his pain, Bliss dares him to be conquered by his need. Laura will touch your heart with this stunning love story.

Last, but certainly not least, in the line-up is **CON MAN** by Maris Soule, LOVESWEPT #635. As head of a foundation that provides money for worthy causes, Kurt Jones is definitely no con man, but he knows that's how Micki Bradford will think of him once she learns of his deception. It all starts when, instead of letting his usual investigator check out a prospective grant recipient, he decides he'll try undercover work himself. He arranges a meeting with expert rider Micki, then on the pretense that he's interested in finding a stable for a horse, pumps her for information . . . even as his gaze caresses her and he longs to touch her as she's never been touched. He's tempted to tell her the truth, to promise he'll never hurt her, but Micki has learned the hard way how irresistible a good-looking liar can be. As Kurt sweeps her into a steamy charade to unearth the facts, Kurt vows he'd dare any danger to win Micki's trust, and teach her to have faith in his love. Maris does nothing less than thrill you with this exciting romance.

On sale this month from Bantam are two thrilling novels of passion and intrigue. First is **LADY VALIANT** by the magnificent Suzanne Robinson, whom *Romantic Times* has described as "an author with star quality." In this mesmerizing tale of grand romantic adventure, Thea Hunt is determined to repay the kindness of Mary, Queen of Scots, by journeying to Scotland to warn her away from a treacherous marriage. But in the thick of an English forest, she suddenly finds herself set upon by thieves . . . and chased down by a golden-haired highwayman who stills her struggles—and stirs her heart—with one penetrating glance from his fiery blue eyes. As a spy in Queen Elizabeth's service, Robin St. John is prepared to despise Thea, whom he considers a traitorous wench, to enjoy her torment as he spirits her away to a castle where she'll remain until Mary Stuart is safely wed. But he finds himself desiring her more than any other woman he's ever met. As captive and captor clash, Robin vows to use his every weapon to make Thea surrender to the raging fires of his need and the rising heat of her own passion.

Lois Wolfe returns with **MASK OF NIGHT,** a tantalizing historical romance where one bewitching actress finds love and danger waiting in the wings. Katie Henslowe's prayers are answered the night wealthy railroad tycoon Julian Gates becomes her benefactor, hiring her family's ragtag acting troupe for his new theater. But no sooner has her uncertain world begun to settle down than the potent kiss of a maddeningly attractive stranger sends her reeling. Matt Dennigan is arrogant, enigmatic, and broke—reasons enough for Katie to avoid him. And when, for secret motives of his own, the mysterious rancher begins to draw her into his search for evidence again Julian, Katie tries to resist. But in Matt's heated embrace she finds herself giving in to her innermost longings, only to discover that she and Matt are trapped in a treacherous quest for justice. Against all odds they become partners in a dangerous mission that will take them from a teeming city to the wild frontier, testing the limits of their courage and turning their fiercest desires into spellbinding love. . . .

Also on sale this month, in the hardcover edition from Doubleday, is **SATIN AND STEELE** by the ever-popular Fayrene Preston. Long out of print, this is a wonderfully evocative and uniquely contemporary love story. Skye Anderson knows the joy and wonder of love, as well as the pain of its tragic loss. She's carved a new life for herself at Dallas's Hayes Corporation, finding security in a cocoon of hardworking days and lonely nights. Then her company is taken over by the legendary corporate raider James Steele, and once again Skye must face the possibility of losing everything she cares about. When Steele enlists her aid in organizing the new corporation, she's determined to prove herself worthy of the challenge. But as they work together side by side, she can't deny that she feels more than a professional interest in her new boss—and that the feeling is mutual. Soon she'll have to decide whether to let go of her desire for Steele once and for all—or to risk everything for a second chance at love.

Happy reading!

With warmest wishes,

Nita Taublib

Associate Publisher

Don't miss these exciting books by your
favorite Bantam authors

On sale in June:
LADY VALIANT
by *Suzanne Robinson*

MASK OF NIGHT
by *Lois Wolfe*

And in hardcover from Doubleday
SATIN AND STEELE
by *Fayrene Preston*

From the bestselling author of
Lady Defiant, Lady Hellfire, and
Lady Gallant . . .

Suzanne Robinson

"An author with star
quality . . . spectacularly talented."
—*Romantic Times*

Lady Valiant

Breathtakingly talented author Suzanne Robinson spins a richly romantic new historical romance set during the spellbinding Elizabethan era. LADY VALIANT is the passionate love story of Rob Savage—highwayman, nobleman, and master spy—and the fiery young beauty he kidnaps.

A tantalizing glimpse follows . . .

The brief stillness vanished as she understood that the man who was more stallion than human was coming for her. Fear lanced through her. She kicked her mare hard and sprang away, racing down the path through the trees. Riding sidesaddle, she had a precarious perch, but she tapped her mare with the crop, knowing that the risk of capture by a highwayman outweigh[ed] the risk of a fall. Her heart pounding with the hoofbeats of her mare, she fled.

The path twisted to the right and she nearly lost her seat as she rounded the turn. Righting herself, she felt the mare stretch her legs out and saw that the way had straightened. She leaned over her horse, not daring to look behind and lose her balance. Thus she only heard the thunder of hooves and felt the spray of dirt as the stallion caught up. The animal's black head appeared, and she kicked her mare in desperation.

A gloved hand appeared, then a golden head. An arm snaked out and encircled her waist. Thea sailed out of the saddle and landed in front of the highwayman. Terror gave her strength. She wriggled and pounded the imprisoning arm.

"None of that, beastly papist gentry mort."

Understanding little of this, caring not at all, Thea wriggled harder and managed to twist so that she could bite the highwayman's arm. She was rewarded with a howl. Twisting again, she bit the hand that snatched at her hair and thrust herself out of the saddle as the stallion was slowing to a trot.

She landed on her side, rolled, and scrambled to her feet. Ahead she could see her mare walking down the trail in search of grass. Sprinting for the animal, she felt her hair come loose from its net and sail out behind her. Only a few yards and she might escape on the mare.

Too late she heard the stallion. She glanced over her shoulder to see a scowling face. She gave a little yelp as a long, lean body sailed at her. She turned to leap out of range, but the highwayman landed on her. The force of his weight jolted the air from her lungs and she fell. The ground jumped at her face. Her head banged against something. There was a moment of sharp pain and the feeling of smothering before she lost her senses altogether.

Her next thought wasn't quite a thought, for in truth there was room in her mind for little more than feeling. Her head ached. She was queasy and she couldn't summon the strength to open her eyes. She could feel her face because someone had laid a palm against her cheek. She could feel her hand, because someone was holding it.

"Wake you, my prize. I've no winding sheet to wrap you in if you die."

The words were harsh. It was the voice of thievery and

rampage, the voice of a masterless man, a highwayman. Her eyes flew open at the thought and met the sun. No, not the sun, bright light filtered through a mane of long, roughly cut tresses. She shifted her gaze to the man's face and saw his lips curve into a smile of combined satisfaction and derision. She could only lie on the ground and blink at him, waiting.

He leaned toward her and she shrank away. Glaring at her, he held her so that she couldn't retreat. He came close, and she was about to scream when he touched the neck of her gown. The feel of his gloved hand on her throat took her voice from her. She began to shake. An evil smile appeared upon his lips, then she felt a tightening of her collar and a rip. She found her voice and screamed as he tore the top button from her gown. Flailing at him weakly, she drew breath to scream again, but he clamped a hand over her mouth.

"Do you want me to stuff my gloves into your mouth?"

She stared at him, trapped by his grip and the malice in his dark blue eyes.

"Do you?"

She shook her head.

"Then keep quiet."

He removed his hand and she squeezed her eyes shut, expecting him to resume his attack. When nothing happened, she peeped at him from beneath her lashes. He was regarding her with a contemptuous look, but soon transferred his gaze to the button in his palm. He pressed it between his fingers, frowned at it, then shoved it into a pouch at his belt.

"I'll have the rest of them later," he said.

Reaching for her, he stopped when she shrank from him. He hesitated, then grinned at her.

"Sit you up by yourself then."

Still waiting for him to pounce on her, she moved her arms, but when she tried to shove herself erect, she found them useless. He snorted. Gathering her in his arms, he raised her to a sitting position. She winced at the pain in her head. His hand came up to cradle her cheek and she moaned.

"If you puke on me I'll tie you face down on your horse for the ride home."

Fear gave way to anger. In spite of her pain, she shoved at his chest. To her chagrin, what she thought were mortal blows turned out to be taps.

"Aaaow! Look what you've done to my lady."

"Get you gone, you old cow. She's well and will remain so, for now. Stubb, put the maid on a horse and let's fly. No sense waiting here for company any longer."

Thea opened her eyes. The highwayman was issuing orders to his ruffians. From her position she could see the day's growth of beard on his chin and the tense cords of muscle in his neck.

"My—my men."

"Will have a long walk," he snapped.

"Leave us," she whispered, trying to sit up. "You have your booty."

The highwayman moved abruptly to kneel in front of her. Taking her by the shoulders, he pulled her so that they faced each other eye to eye.

"But Mistress Hunt, you are the booty. All the rest is fortune's addition."

"But—"

He ignored her. Standing quickly, he picked her up. Made dizzy by the sudden change, she allowed her head to drop to his shoulder. She could smell the leather of his jerkin and feel the soft cambric of his shirt. An outlaw who wore cambric shirts.

She was transferred to the arms of another ruffian, a wiry man no taller than she with a crooked nose and a belligerent expression. Her captor mounted the black stallion again and reached down.

"Give her to me."

Lifted in front of the highwayman, she was settled in his lap a great distance from the ground. The stallion danced sideways and his master put a steadying hand on the animal's neck. The stallion calmed at once.

"Now, Mistress Hunt, shall I tie your hands, or will you behave? I got no patience for foolish gentry morts who don't know better than to try outrunning horses."

Anger got the better of her. "You may be sure the next time I leave I'll take your horse."

"God's blood, woman. You take him, and I'll give you the whipping you've asked for."

His hand touched a whip tied to his saddle and she believed him. She screamed and began to struggle.

"Cease your nattering, woman."

He fastened his hand over her mouth again. His free arm wrapped around her waist. Squeezing her against his hard body, he stifled her cries. When she went limp from lack of air, he released her.

"Any more yowling and I'll gag you."

Grabbing her by the shoulders, he drew her close so that she was forced to look into his eyes. Transfixed by their scornful beauty, she remained silent.

"What say you?" he asked. "Shall I finish what I began and take all your buttons?"

Hardly able to draw breath, she hadn't the strength to move her lips.

"Answer, woman. Will you ride quietly, or fight beneath me on the ground again?"

"R—ride."

Chuckling he turned her around so that her back was to his chest and called to his men. The outlaw called Stubb rode up leading a horse carrying Hobby, and Thea twisted her head around to see if her maid fared well.

"Look here, Rob Savage," Stubb said. "If you want to scrap with the gentry mort all day, I'm going on. No telling when someone else is going to come along, and I'm not keen on another fight this day."

"Give me a strap then."

A strap. He was going to beat her. Thea gasped and rammed her elbow into Rob's stomach. She writhed and twisted, trying to escape the first blow from the lash. Rob finally trapped her by fastening his arms about her and holding her arms to her body.

"Quick, Stubb, tie her hands with the strap."

Subsiding, Thea bit her lower lip. Her struggles had been for naught. Rob's arm left her, but he shook her by the shoulders.

"Now be quiet or I'll tie you to a pack horse."

"Aaaow! Savage, Robin Savage, the highwayman. God preserve us. We're lost, lost. Oh, mistress, it's Robin Savage. He's killed hundreds of innocent souls. He kills babes and ravages their mothers and steals food from children and burns churches and dismembers clergymen and—"

Thea felt her body grow cold and heavy at the same time. She turned and glanced up at the man who held her. He was frowning at the hysterical Hobby. Suddenly he looked down at her. One of his brows lifted and he smiled slowly.

"A body's got to have a calling."

"You—you've done these things?"

"Now how's a man to remember every little trespass and sin, especially a man as busy as me?"

He grinned at her, lifted a hand to his men, and kicked the stallion. Her head was thrown back against his chest. He steadied her with an arm around her waist, but she squirmed away from him. He ignored her efforts and pulled her close as the horse sprang into a gallop. She grasped his arm with her bound hands, trying to pry it loose to no avail. It was as much use for a snail to attempt to move a boulder.

The stallion leaped over a fallen sapling and she clutched at Savage's arm. Riding a small mare was a far less alarming experience than trying to keep her seat on this black giant. She would have to wait for a chance to escape, but escape she must.

As they rode, Thea mastered her fears enough to begin to think. This man wanted more than just riches and rape. If he'd only wanted these things, he could have finished his attack when he'd begun it. And it wasn't as if she were tempting to men, a beauty worth keeping. She'd found that out long ago in France. And this Savage knew her name. The mystery calmed her somewhat. Again she twisted, daring a glance at him.

"Why have you abducted me?"

He gaped at her for a moment before returning his gaze to the road ahead. "For the same reason I take any woman. For using."

He slowed the stallion and turned off the road. Plunging into the forest, they left behind the men assigned to bring the coach and wagons. Several thieves went ahead, while Stubb and the rest followed their master. Thea summoned her courage to break the silence once more.

"Why else?"

"What?"

"It can't be the only reason, to, to . . ."

"Why not?"

"You know my name. You were looking for me, not for just anyone."

"Is that so?"

"Are you going to hold me for ransom? There are far richer prizes than me."

"Ransom. Now there's a right marvelous idea. Holding a woman for ransom's a pleasureful occupation."

As he leered down at her, fear returned. Her body shook. She swallowed and spoke faintly.

"No."

There was a sharp gasp of exasperation from Savage. "Don't you be telling me what I want."

"But you can't."

His gaze ran over her face and hair. The sight appeared to anger him, for he cursed and snarled at her.

"Don't you be telling me what I can do. God's blood, woman, I could throw you down and mount you right here."

She caught her lower lip between her teeth, frozen into her own horror by his threats. He snarled at her again and turned her away from him, holding her shoulders so that she couldn't face him. Though he used only the strength of his hands, it was enough to control her, which frightened her even more.

"I could do it," he said. "I might if you don't keep quiet. Mayhap being mounted a few times would shut you up."

Thea remained silent, not daring to anger him further. She had no experience of villains. This one had hurt her. He might hurt her worse. She must take him at his word, despite her suspicion that he'd planned to hold her for ransom. She must escape. She must escape with Hobby and find her men.

As dusk fell they crossed a meadow and climbed a rounded hill. At the top she had a view of the countryside. Before her stretched a great forest, its trees so thick she could see nothing but an ocean of leaves.

Savage led his men down the hillside and into the forest. As they entered, the sun faded into a twilight caused by the canopy of leaves about them. Savage rode on until the twilight had almost vanished. Halting in a clearing by a noisy stream, he lifted Thea down.

She'd been on the horse so long and the hours of fear had wearied her so much that her legs buckled under her. Savage caught her, his hands coming up under her arms, and she stumbled against him. Clutching her, he swore. She looked up at him to find him glaring at her again. She caught her breath, certain he would leap upon her.

His arms tightened about her, but he didn't throw her to the ground. Instead, he stared at her. Too confused at the moment to be afraid, she stared back. Long moments passed while they gazed at each other, studying, wary, untrusting.

When he too seemed caught in a web of reverie her fears gradually eased. Eyes of gentian blue met hers and she felt a stab of pain. To her surprise, looking at him had caused the pain.

Until that moment she hadn't realized a man's mere appearance could delight to the point of pain.

It was her first long look at him free of terror. Not in all her years in the fabulous court of France had she seen such a man. Even his shoulders were muscled. They were wide in contrast to his hips and he was taller than any Frenchman. He topped any of his thievish minions and yet seemed unaware of the effect of his appearance. Despite his angelic coloring, however, he had the disposition of an adder. He was scowling at her, as if something had caught him unprepared and thus annoyed him. Wariness and fear rushed to the fore again.

"Golden eyes and jet black hair. Why did you have to be so—God's blood, woman." He thrust her away from him. "Never you mind. You were right anyway, little papist. I'm after ransom."

Bewildered, she remained where she was while he stalked away from her. He turned swiftly to point at her.

"Don't you think of running. If I have to chase you and wrestle with you again, you'll pay in any way I find amusing." He marched off to shout ill-tempered orders at his men.

Hobby trotted up to her and began untying the leather strap that bound her hands. Thea stared at Robin Savage, frightened once more and eyeing his leather-clad figure. How could she have forgotten his cruelty and appetite simply because he had a lush, well-formed body and eyes that could kindle wet leaves? She watched him disappear into the trees at the edge of the clearing, and at last she was released from the bondage of his presence.

"He's mad," she said.

"Mad, of course, he's mad," Hobby said. "He's a thief and a murderer and a ravager."

"How could God create such a man, so—so pleasing to the eye and so evil of spirit?"

"Take no fantasy about this one, mistress. He's a foul villain who'd as soon slit your throat as spit on you."

"I know." Thea bent and whispered to Hobby. "Can you run fast and long? We must fly this night. Who knows what will happen to us once he's done settling his men."

"I can run."

"Good. I'll watch for my chance and you do as well." She looked around at the men caring for horses and making a fire. Stubb watched them as he unloaded saddlebags. "For now, I must find privacy."

Hobby pointed to a place at the edge of the clearing where bushes grew thick. They walked toward it unhindered. Hobby stopped at the edge of the clearing to guard Thea's retreat. Thea plunged into the trees looking for the thickest bushes. Thrusting a low-hanging branch aside, she rounded an oak tree. A tall form blocked her way. Before she could react, she was thrust against the tree, and a man's body pressed against hers.

Robin Savage held her fast, swearing at her. She cast a frightened glance at him, but he wasn't looking at her. He was absorbed in studying her lips. His anger had faded and his expression took on a somnolent turbulence. He leaned close and whispered in her ear, sending chills down her spine.

"Running away in spite of my warnings, little papist."

Thea felt a leg shove between her thighs. His chest pressed against her breasts, causing her to pant. He stared into her eyes and murmured.

"Naughty wench. Now I'll have to punish you."

Mask of Night
by
Lois Wolfe

author of *The Schemers*

A spectacular new historical romance that combines breath-taking intrigue and suspense with breathless passion.

She was an actress who made her living spinning dreams. He was a rancher turned spy whose dreams had all been bitterly broken. Against all odds, they became partners in a danger-ous mission that would take them from the teeming city to the wild frontier, testing the limits of their courage, and turning their fiercest desires into spellbinding love . . .

Read on for a taste of this unforgettable tale.

What use Gates might have for Katie was immediately apparent when Matt saw her emerge from the cloakroom in an under-stated emerald green gown. He made note of the dress, espe-cially the top of it, the part that wasn't there. Nice swoop.

Real nice swoop.

Other men noticed too, as she crossed the lobby to the front desk. Matt debated following her. He was already late for dinner with the Senator, but, hell, a little more close observation couldn't hurt.

He joined her at the front desk. Her expression showed annoyance the moment she saw him, and he guessed she regret-ted trying to be polite to him.

"Looks like we both have business here," he said, leaning on the counter.

She turned her back on him, leaving him free to study her, the indignant thrust of her shoulders, the fragile trough of her spine. A wisp of dark golden hair had escaped its pin and rested in the curve of her neck.

"I'm here to meet my brother, Edmund Henslowe," she told the desk clerk.

The clerk went off to check the message boxes. She cocked her chin to her shoulder and sent Matt a withering look.

Hazel, he thought. Her eyes were hazel, more green than brown.

"Miss Katie Henslowe?" the clerk asked when he returned. "Mr. Henslowe wishes you to join him in his suite."

She was obviously startled. "His suite? Here?"

"Sixth floor. Number nineteen."

Six nineteen, Matt thought, looking ahead and not at her.

"Thank you." Icy, perfunctory. She was miffed.

The clerk had business at the other end of the long front desk, and they were alone for a moment.

She stood silent awhile, then turned to Matt. "Did you get all that?"

He was cautious. "What?"

"Don't play dumb. It looks too natural on you. Nice piece of news, wasn't it? The fact that my brother has a room here? Makes it seem like he has money, doesn't it? Well, let me assure you, you and whichever of our creditors you're the snoop for, Poppy does *not* have funds to make payments."

Matt played along, glancing around the opulent lobby. "This doesn't exactly look like a place for the destitute."

"I know." She backed down, stiffly. "Just, please, try to understand. My brother is here only to develop resources for the troupe. Now, I'm sure your loan department will be glad to hear that we may have the potential to resume quarterly payments." She paused. "You *are* a bank agent for Philadelphia Savings, aren't you?"

He shook his head.

"New York Fiduciary?"

"No."

"You work in the private sector, then, for an individual?"

"You could say that."

She looked away. "It's about Edmund, isn't it?"

"How'd you guess?"

Her glance took in his unfashionable attire and worn shoes. "My brother tends to attract an eclectic and, sometimes, illicit crowd."

"Which one am I? Eclectic or illicit?"

"You're a coward and a spy, and I doubt that you've got enough grapeshot in the bag to so much as fire off your name."

He looked at her for a long time. "Insults like that don't come from a lady."

"No." She held his gaze. "And they don't apply to a gentleman."

"Look, I'm not one of your brother's Jack Nasty lowlifes."

"You're not? And yet you have business here?" She studied him thoughtfully. "Are you meeting the senator then?"

Christ, how'd she know? He felt himself grow stony-faced, trying to keep reaction to a minimum.

"I remember," she went on, "seeing you waylay the distinguished senator backstage, Mr. . . . ?" She waited again for his name.

"Nasty," he said curtly. "Jack Nasty."

"I thought so."

To his surprise, she sidled close and put a hand on his arm. "Sir?" she called to the desk clerk. "My friend here has a request."

Matt tensed. What was she doing?

"Yes, sir?" the clerk asked, returning to them.

"He needs his messages," Katie interjected before Matt could speak.

"Of course." The clerk turned to Matt. "What is the name?"

Damn her.

She smiled prettily at him. "Now, come on. Don't dawdle," she said, as to a child. "You'll make us both late."

He hated being manipulated. He especially hated a woman who did it so well.

She patted his hand. "I know you've had a terrible sore throat." She turned to the clerk. "Maybe if you could just lean close, so he can whisper."

The clerk looked dubious, but obligingly leaned over the counter.

Matt felt pressure rise inside him like steam in a boiler.

"Still hurts?" she asked. "Would it be easier if you just spell it? I'm sure—"

"Dennigan!" The word shot out from between gritted teeth.

The clerk stared, astonished.

Katie removed her hand from his. "See how much better you sound when you try?" she said, then turned to the clerk. "Please check the message box for Mr. Dennigan."

Matt leaned close so no one would see him grab her wrist, grab it hard. "Dennigan," he repeated. "Matt Dennigan."

"Charmed, I'm sure."

She jerked her arm free as the clerk returned. His manner was noticeably more unctuous toward Matt. "Mr. Dennigan? It seems Senator Cahill is waiting dinner for you in the Walker Room."

"The Walker Room," Katie said. "Isn't that the salon for very private dining?"

The clerk nodded again. "Yes, ma'am. Right through the arch and turn left."

Katie looked at Matt. "Well, now, Matt, enjoy your dinner."

She was gracious in triumph, almost sweet, he thought, as she left him. She hurried to the elevator foyer. He stood a long while, watching until the accordion gate of the elevator collapsed sideways to let her on.

She had taken his amateurish game of sleuth and, in one polished play, raised the ante to life-or-death for the Senator's investigation. If she dared mention Matt Dennigan and Senator Cahill in the same breath to the cutthroat millionaire she was about to meet, the game was over. Julian Gates would run for cover and retaliate with all the congressional influence—and hired guns—his money could buy.

Jesus Christ.

CALL JAN SPILLER'S ASTROLINE

OFFICIAL RULES

To enter the sweepstakes below carefully follow all instructions found elsewhere in this offer.

The **Winners Classic** will award prizes with the following approximate maximum values: 1 Grand Prize: $26,500 (or $25,000 cash alternate); 1 First Prize: $3,000; 5 Second Prizes: $400 each; 35 Third Prizes: $100 each; 1,000 Fourth Prizes: $7.50 each. Total maximum retail value of Winners Classic Sweepstakes is $42,500. Some presentations of this sweepstakes may contain individual entry numbers corresponding to one or more of the aforementioned prize levels. To determine the Winners, individual entry numbers will first be compared with the winning numbers preselected by computer. For winning numbers not returned, prizes will be awarded in random drawings from among all eligible entries received. Prize choices may be offered at various levels. If a winner chooses an automobile prize, all license and registration fees, taxes, destination charges and, other expenses not offered herein are the responsibility of the winner. If a winner chooses a trip, travel must be complete within one year from the time the prize is awarded. Minors must be accompanied by an adult. Travel companion(s) must also sign release of liability. Trips are subject to space and departure availability. Certain black-out dates may apply.

The following applies to the sweepstakes named above:

No purchase necessary. You can also enter the sweepstakes by sending your name and address to: P.O. Box 508, Gibbstown, N.J. 08027. Mail each entry separately. Sweepstakes begins 6/1/93. Entries must be received by 12/30/94. Not responsible for lost, late, damaged, misdirected, illegible or postage due mail. Mechanically reproduced entries are not eligible. All entries become property of the sponsor and will not be returned.

Prize Selection/Validations: Selection of winners will be conducted no later than 5:00 PM on January 28, 1995, by an independent judging organization whose decisions are final. Random drawings will be held at 1211 Avenue of the Americas, New York, N.Y. 10036. Entrants need not be present to win. Odds of winning are determined by total number of entries received. Circulation of this sweepstakes is estimated not to exceed 200 million. All prizes are guaranteed to be awarded and delivered to winners. Winners will be notified by mail and may be required to complete an affidavit of eligibility and release of liability which must be returned within 14 days of date on notification or alternate winners will be selected in a random drawing. Any prize notification letter or any prize returned to a participating sponsor, Bantam Doubleday Dell Publishing Group, Inc., its participating divisions or subsidiaries, or the independent judging organization as undeliverable will be awarded to an alternate winner. Prizes are not transferable. No substitution for prizes except as offered or as may be necessary due to unavailability, in which case a prize of equal or greater value will be awarded. Prizes will be awarded approximately 90 days after the drawing. All taxes are the sole responsibility of the winners. Entry constitutes permission (except where prohibited by law) to use winners' names, hometowns, and likenesses for publicity purposes without further or other compensation. Prizes won by minors will be awarded in the name of parent or legal guardian.

Participation: Sweepstakes open to residents of the United States and Canada, except for the province of Quebec. Sweepstakes sponsored by Bantam Doubleday Dell Publishing Group, Inc., (BDD), 1540 Broadway, New York, NY 10036. Versions of this sweepstakes with different graphics and prize choices will be offered in conjunction with various solicitations or promotions by different subsidiaries and divisions of BDD. Where applicable, winners will have their choice of any prize offered at level won. Employees of BDD, its divisions, subsidiaries, advertising agencies, independent judging organization, and their immediate family members are not eligible.

Canadian residents, in order to win, must first correctly answer a time limited arithmetical skill testing question. Void in Puerto Rico, Quebec and wherever prohibited or restricted by law. Subject to all federal, state, local and provincial laws and regulations. For a list of major prize winners (available after 1/29/95): send a self-addressed, stamped envelope entirely separate from your entry to: Sweepstakes Winners, P.O. Box 517, Gibbstown, NJ 08027. Requests must be received by 12/30/94. DO NOT SEND ANY OTHER CORRESPONDENCE TO THIS P.O. BOX.